Obsidian Wolf

A short novel by

Sampson Hammer Stinson

Strategic Book Publishing and Rights Co.

Strategic Book Publishing and Rights Co.
12620 FM 1960, Suite A4-507
Houston TX 77065
www.spbra.com

ISBN: 978-1-61897-442-6

For my family.

Your love and support has made this dream come true.

Chapter 1

Vast and empty... azure majestic... lifeless abyss...

***

Rook Evrett imagined two would-be novelists tackling one another and wrestling in a Bugs Bunny cloud of dust behind the steering mechanism of his mind. The novelists were the embodiment of Rook's creative process, and from their posts in his imagination, they had accomplished nothing. The blank screen in front of Rook had stumped them all.

As much as Rook enjoyed his playful projections of King and Koontz, they weren't helping him. All he had for his "story" was a pilfered Stephen King villain, Mr. Grey. Rook had a gift—or a curse, depending on how you looked at it—that attached him to the characters of *Dreamcatcher*. In tribute and out of respect for the author that had created a fantasy similar to his reality, Rook wanted to give Grey new life.

Originally an alien hell bent on destroying the world, Grey would be reborn as a new character, equally malevolent, but not an alien. He envisioned Grey as a cold, calculated killer from within. He would be a surfacing personality inside an otherwise normal and well adjusted man—the murderous impulse inside us all with the voice that makes us wonder what it would be like to run over the jogger who insists on using the street when a perfectly good sidewalk mere feet away lies unused. Grey would be the embodiment of that evil, growing like cancer in some poor sap, and would hopefully grow into a new character unto himself.

Unfortunately, what things boiled down to was a refried antagonist who he hadn't yet named, a couple of secondary meat-bags for the slaughter, and a gaping hole where a protagonist ought to be. The poor sap protagonist was an evasive one.

Rook pushed his fingers through his shaggy brown hair. He was average height for a man, but his lanky figure made him seem taller than he really was. Despite the bachelor diet of Ramen noodles, mac and cheese, and frozen pizza, with an occasional healthy item sprinkled in, he maintained an almost gaunt figure. Due to a metabolism that could rival a hummingbird's, he constantly snacked and was on first-name basis with the clerks at the local grocery.

He imagined Grey standing behind the two fighting writers, watching, grinning in darkness. Grey observed King and Koontz silently from between bookshelves, shadow cast over his face. Behind the control center was a full library, books cataloging everything about Rook's life. There was every sight, smell, taste, every book he ever read, every memory ever repressed, every scraped knee, every hopped fence, broken window, high school crush, fishing trip, episode of *Boy Meets World*. Everything Rook had every known, loved, or hated was present and accounted for.

Grey waited patiently in the endless aisles of knowledge and nonsense. He twirled something in the fingertips of one hand; it was small, metallic, and sheathed in an elaborately carved jade holster. It was the pocketknife Rook's "father" threatened him not to touch, the pocketknife Rook stole and accidentally stabbed Justin Thomas with in fifth grade. Grey flicked it open. Click. He flicked it back into its jaded home. Click. The eagle carved in the side screamed. Open, click. A fire burned behind Grey's eyes, malicious, malevolent. He stepped forward, toward the two now resting with their backs against the controls. Click. The shadows fell away from his face. Click.

His face . . . his face was a problem. What face would inspire the appropriate fear and convey the level of evil within? The simple solution was to allow Grey to choose his own form and let evil be evil.

Contented with the mind-blowingly miniscule progress he'd made, Rook sat back in his chair, stretched his arms, and looked out the window at the waning sunset.

"Let's go for a walk, Tank."

A large chocolate lab peacefully snoozing on an old blanket in the corner perked up. He raised his enormous head and shook himself awake. With a quick stretch of the front legs, then the back, he trotted over to Rook's side and gave him the "Well?" look.

"Grab your leash."

With a disgruntled huff Tank went and retrieved his leash off an end table near the front door. The cabin was small, but it suited Rook. The front door led directly into his dual living room/office. There was a small kitchen, a single bedroom, and a tiny bathroom as well, all cleanly kept. Rook figured there were probably larger studio apartments.

He modestly furnished it with a second-hand couch, a couple of end tables, a heavy oak coffee table he'd lucked into, a Wal-Mart-brand black desk, which was already cracked, a thirty-year-old entertainment center with bookshelves crammed full of movies on either side, and a brand new pillow-top-over-memory-foam bed. Sleep was sacred to him. He'd also sprung for the specially placed satellite dish so he could get internet access on his laptop, and carefully perched atop the entertainment center was a forty-inch flat-screen LCD TV with a family of game consoles stacked in the shelves beneath. He enjoyed the isolation of nature but wouldn't deprive himself of modern luxuries.

He stood and did a stretch of his own as Tank returned and dropped the leash at his feet with a disgruntled snort.

"You really don't like that thing, do you?" He bent over, grabbed Tank's head so that his skin rolled forward and bunched up, and kissed the soft fur between his eyes. "I'll let you go commando if you promise not to stray. Got it?"

Tank's tongue lapped out of his squished face and caught Rook on his.

"All right, let's go." Rook tried to spit the taste away as he stood up.

Tank immediately took off down the front steps when

7

the door was opened.

"Tank!" The dog stopped midway to the woods and sat impatiently.

Rook savored the cool, crisp air as he slid on his hoodie and ambled toward the path down where Tank was anxiously staring. Southern Oregon fall was under way. The regularly green landscape was beginning to pepper orange and brown and the Pacific Winds were getting colder. A few more weeks and the first frost would arrive to give winter a foothold.

"Let's go off the beaten path today, shall we?" Rook walked north from the cabin rather than their usual Eastern path. Plant growth was receding for the year and allowed access to previously unmanageable areas. Spruce and mountain hemlock, Douglas firs, and an occasional Pine tree stood tall and full.

Tank merrily trotted no more than six feet ahead, easily navigating brush and marking nearly every tree. Before long he'd be empty and resolve to simply lifting a leg near trees. He sniffed around, kicking up dust and dirt under the sea of leaves, needles, and random decay.

Rook let his creative side absorb the sensations as they walked. He watched fading sunlight trickling through the trees. He carefully studied a fat orb-weaver's web and tried to imagine what unfortunate insect was cocooned in a silk coffin as a snack for later. When Tank chased a red squirrel up a tree and snarled underneath, Rook listened to the squirrel cussing him out from the safety of an overhanging branch. The squirrel's fluffy red tail twitched in rhythm with the angry chirping.

Rook lost track of time and let the outside world disappear, as he often did. The mangled remains of a particularly plump western sage grouse snapped him out of the daze. Tank sniffed them carefully and turned them with his nose. There were gray wolves in the area, but something about the carcass didn't seem right. As Rook examined it, he realized what was missing, or rather what wasn't missing. All the meat, tissue, and organs, while shredded, were present. The creature wasn't killed for food by some wild predator. It was torn apart either for some sick sense of sport or simply for the pleasure of it.

"It's getting dark, pal. We'd better head back." He gave Tank a pat and a pet before realizing that Tank was no longer staring at the mutilated grouse. His attention had shifted toward a tree a couple feet in front of them. He was in the beginning rumbles of a growl.

There was no movement by the tree, just a small pile of leaves and forest debris at the base. Tank remained rigid and in stance, growling. Rook stepped toward the tree and Tank looked at him with a whimper. Burning curiosity pushed Rook forward regardless. His feet, betraying him, sent him to the ground. His hand landed with a squish in the bloody remains. As he pushed himself back up, damning his feet, he noticed from a ground-level view there was a hollow in the base of the tree.

He scooted over to it, still on all fours, and pushed the debris aside. Near the roots was an opening. He couldn't tell if it was a natural space between roots or if it had been carved out. As his hands cleared the opening, Tank's growls became more intense. There was something in there and Tank knew it. Rook had to know, too. The unseen, undeniable force that was curiosity tethered him to whatever was beneath the tree with excited energy like an underground power line.

Casting aside all his better judgments, Rook kept clearing the opening of leaves, twigs, dirt, pinecones, and then something hard and smooth. He had half-expected some critter that had startled Tank to bite him. Instead, his fingers wrapped around a solid, lifeless, and oddly warm object. The heat turned to a comfortable burn, sending confused nerve signals racing to his brain. It was hotter than anything out there should be, but the warmth was inviting and spread through his hand and up his arm.

When he finally pulled the object out, he was amazed to find it was an obsidian carving of a wolf with an odd luminescence to it. It almost seemed to glow, even in the dwindling sunlight. He would've expected to find something like this beaten up, faded, and worn by time, but its smooth, black surface still shined.

9

Rook had seen the old obsidian flows in the mountains, but something about this piece was remarkable.

Rook was so enthralled by the find that he didn't see Tank charging. The Labrador latched onto his arm and knocked the figurine to the ground. He tried to push Tank away and pull his arm back. Tank carefully released his grip and stood watching. The skin hadn't been broken. If Tank wanted to, he could've torn him limb from limb. Instead, Rook had been struck with a quick, precise blow.

"What the hell was that?!" Rook questioned the animal angrily and stood, preparing to strike. The standard survivor's adrenaline rush was tainted with an extra edge of primal rage that was nearly blinding.

A little projector flipped on in the back of Rook's mind and he saw Tank as a pup, curled up in small wicker basket cushioned with red fleece blankets. Tank was centered between his siblings and looked like a fluffy bon-bon the way he was rolled up. Rook remembered how Tank had stretched a tiny paw out, with its infantile, soft claws, yawned, and then cracked an eye open to examine the man staring at him. They watched each other silently for thirty seconds before Tank once more closed his eyes and burrowed his head into the five-dog mass of fur.

Frozen in striking stance, staring at the dog, the anger slowly dissipated from Rook and disappeared with the same mystery as it had arrived. He unclenched his fist and dropped it to his side. He had never hit a dog, nor did he ever want to. In the heat of the moment he had raised his fist against Tank and was terrified that he had done so. Luckily Tank could melt an iceberg with his "puppy" face. Normally used to acquire treats, the "puppy" face said much more this time. Tank looked up at him with soft, soulful eyes, telling him, as best he could, that he would never *really* hurt him.

"Sorry, bud. But you did just bite me." Rook chuckled and gave Tank an ear flopping. He spoke to Tank just as he would anyone else and never questioned the sanity of it. Tank was a truer companion than any other friend he'd ever had. "Why did you do that, huh?"

He examined the saliva-stained sleeve of his hoodie for holes or tears. There was nothing. Tank had been forceful in the shake but gentle in the bite. The figurine lay on the ground in front of him. He went to pick it up, but Tank growled again.

"All right, I get it. I won't touch it. But we can't very well leave a find like that here, can we?" Rook thought for a moment. "I'll just use my *slobber-covered* sleeve to pick it up and put it in this front pocket," he narrated to Tank as he picked it up. "Is that okay? I wouldn't want to upset your delicate dog sensibilities." Tank huffed unhappily but conceded.

During the walk home Tank never left his side. He looked up at Rook repeatedly with mournful eyes. Rook could tell he was sorry for biting but that some-thing troubled the dog. Tank nuzzled his hand on a few occasions and garnered affection each time.

When they returned, Rook pulled his hoodie off and threw it over the couch without taking the figurine out of the front pocket. Tank did a round through the house, sniffed his kibble for any changes, and plopped contentedly down on his blanket in the corner.

Rook pulled a Coors from the fridge and grabbed the TV remote. He quickly found what he'd DVRed and collapsed into the couch. After an hour of watching the abrasive Dr. House save lives, he began to eye the hoodie. He had found some mysterious wolf whittled out of obsidian under a tree in the middle of the woods. It required attention.

Tank watched him suspiciously as he reached into the pocket. Rook took it out cautiously, trying not to get the dog started again. "See? It's just a statue." He examined it carefully. The wolf was intricately carved in a striking stance. Its head was lowered, its teeth were barely showing but clearly defined in a snarl, and its eyes were calculating. It looked as if the creature had been frozen in the seconds before making a kill. The eyes were picking the prey apart and analyzing every weakness. The kill had been made before the wolf even moved.

His arm began to tingle with warmth again. It spread up past the elbow, through the bicep and tricep, and into the deltoid muscle of his shoulder. This time he set the figurine down himself. "You're right, Tank. That's just too weird. We'll go in to town tomorrow and ask Jon what he makes of it."

Tank relaxed his gaze and curled back up in his blanket. Rook lay back and closed his eyes. The fading tingle in his arm made him stretch and wiggle his fingers. He slowly drifted away on the couch. He drifted away from the cabin, away from the woods, away from the world, away from everything.

Chapter 2

In many of his dreams he found himself inside his own mind with his characters. Rook would chat it up with Daniel Death from his Reaper series, Charlie and the gang from a werewolf story, the nameless "boy" from his short stories, King and Koontz, Barnabas, Cissa, Cain, any character that visited. Once he'd had a dream where, in conversation with Charlie, he was rudely interrupted by Captain Crunch spouting off incessantly about his cereal. He then promptly awoke from his sleep, grabbed his feeding trough, a large green serving bowl he used for his above-average appetite, and sloshed it full of milk and Crunch.

As inspiring and sometimes influential as his dreams were, he recognized them for the subconscious flounder they were. He was able to experience dreams in a way nobody else could and had been able to do so ever since the wreck. Only the boys from *Dreamcatcher* came close with their library. Talking to a college-aged grim reaper and a cartoon cereal peddler was weird, but he was aware. He could wander through his own mind at will and manifest his thoughts, thoughts like his characters. He knew it wasn't real, but it always felt real. When he finally drifted to his mind's library on the couch, things were different.

Normally his characters would greet him in the library, coming and going as they pleased, but the library was silent. The shelves of nervous hands, proper door assembly, third-grade lunches, driver's ed, and endless trivia all sat in darkness. No one was present to peruse the aisles, to share jokes, to question plot points. The only light issued from the front of the room near the viewing window. From his vantage point near the end of an aisle he could see the control area, too, was empty and that nothingness waited behind the window.

He spoke softly to himself, "This is going to be a boring dream."

He sat behind the control panel in a computer chair and spun around in circles. Closing his eyes, he tried to force his dream elsewhere. "C'mon, Bahamas with Dawn." The quiet inside his head was unsettling. An evening trapped in a library full of books he already knew front to back would be painfully boring. He squeezed his eyes tighter and focused on the sandy beach, cloudless skies, and azure expanse of ocean.

Dawn was next to him in a skimpy red bikini laid back in a lounge chair. Her frame was petite, but her figure was curved in the perfect hourglass shape. Her skin was soft and flowery, her bosom was large and perky, her waist was narrow, and her butt was tiny but tight. Rook had spent plenty of time examining the real Dawn and didn't think the dream was too exaggerated. If anything, it didn't do her justice; nothing could. There was a spark in her even his imagination couldn't capture.

When she turned to face him, her long, smooth, dark brunette hair slid over her shoulders. She was wearing large black sunglasses. She had never worn sunglasses in any of the ways he envisioned her. He wanted to see her blue eyes. She slowly removed the glasses on his thought. Her warm smile suddenly seemed mocking and complacent. Above the smirk her eyes were torn out. Empty, bloodied sockets stared back at him.

Rook gasped and opened his eyes as the chair came to a stop.

"Ahahahaha." A pleased cackle slithered out from somewhere in the aisles.

He had never been brought back to the library before. His dreams were linear as he navigated through them. To be brought back was out of his control. He stood up and inched cautiously toward one of the aisles.

"Which one of you is here?"

Suddenly addressing subconscious creations seemed ludicrous. He stared down one dark aisle after another, longing to be back on the beach with *his* Dawn. As he approached the particularly bulky aisle recording every movie he'd ever seen, the silence was broken.

"This is interesting . . ."

Rook didn't recognize the voice. It was heavy and raspy, unlike any character he'd ever allowed into his dreams. He did know where it was coming from: a dusty section tucked away in the very back of the great library. He hated those shelves and every page of information they held.

"Come heeere, Rook." The words were as inviting as the hiss of a cobra and seemed to scrape out of the darkness.

He reluctantly walked toward the source of the voice. The light didn't reach to the section, but Rook knew whoever was back there was reading things that were in the dark for a reason. He could see a tall figure faced toward a shelf with a book in hand. Long and slender fingers turned pages rapidly. They looked like talons scratching at flat bones. The man had a crooked smile that cut through the darkness.

Rook focused hard on the beach once more, straining to leave the dark section of the library behind.

"That won't work."

"What do you mean?" Rook didn't want to ask questions. He wanted to be rid of this intruder and get back to his peaceful, controlled dreams.

"You're trying to go back to the beach." The man remained smiling, facing the book.

As Rook examined him, he realized the man wasn't complete. Rather than feet planted on the floor, his legs disappeared in shadows that rooted out like tentacles in the darkness. Rook stepped around, looking for a face, and instead found that there were no eyes or distinguishable features above the yellow-toothed grin. Only more dark tendrils waited to be found, wriggling above the half face, attempting to thread together features and vaguely producing a cranial structure.

"Who are you?"

15

"Who do you want me to be?" The tentacles forming his head quivered. The creature had turned to face him and the smile was even more contorted. The corners of the mouth curved wickedly and extended well into where cheekbones ought to be. "C'mon, Rookie. Who should I be?!" Transparent, black saliva seeped out of the mouth with each word.

Chapter 3

Morning rays slid through the cabin's windows and ran across the room. Tank nuzzled Rook and squeezed his head under his owner's arm. Feeling the movement and presence, Rook opened his eyes just in time to see a long, pink tongue slap him in the face.

"Dammit, Tank." He groggily sat up, rubbed his eyes, and glanced at the clock. "It's six in the morning, dog." He laid back into the couch and put his arms over his head, blocking the upper half of his face from the light. He thought about his nightmare and tried to remember anything more before he had slipped into deep sleep and things went black. The only image that came to him was that of Dawn and her empty eye sockets.

Tank squeezed his snout under Rook's elbow once more.

"Oh no, you don't," he said, sitting back up before Tank could snake him another lap. "Let's go outside."

Tank wagged his tail so ferociously that his hindquarters bounced in rhythm. He ran to the door and scratched just under the knob.

"Knock that off. You're gonna scratch up the door." Rook's left hand touched something hard and smooth between the couch cushions. It was the wolf. He pulled it out from the crevice and examined it once more. The odd heat wasn't with the figurine anymore, though it still had an eerie menace to it. He remembered placing it on the end table before falling asleep. He must have knocked it onto the couch.

Tank whined.

"All right, Jeezus." He walked toward the door that

did, in fact, have scratches gouged in below the knob. "Have I ever told you that you have terrible morning breath?" He wiped his mouth once more and reached for the doorknob, but it moved on its own before he touched it. Tank switched from sitting to standing impatiently while Rook hesitantly put his eye to the peephole.

With a loud knock Deputy Tatum said, "Yo, Rook! It's me."

Rook sighed with relief. "You scared the shit out of me, Tatum."

Tank ran out the door as soon as Rook had opened it and spent little time sniffing Tatum before going to attend to his business. In the few years Rook had been in Kyruht, Tatum had become one of his better human friends. He had recently made the force after Deputy Driggs's unfortunate misfire. While young and lacking experience, he was abundant in enthusiasm and book learning.

"What are you doing here at six in the morning?"

"Good to see you, too. Mind if I come in? It's not exactly toasty out here." Tatum bounced on his heels and rubbed his hands.

"Pussy. It's not even to freezing point yet."

"Yeah, but it's getting there. It's dropped at least fifteen since last night." Tatum shivered.

Rook sighed. "C'mon in," he said and stepped aside from the door.

"You got anything to drink? Some hot coffee maybe?"

"Why, yes, sir. I can whip some hot coffee right up for you. Is there anything else you want? I could make some fresh cinnamon rolls, massage your feet, wipe your ass."

Tatum said, "You would like that, wouldn't you?"

"You know, the gay jokes never get old. Why don't you come up with something else?" They played the insult game nearly every time they were together.

"That wasn't a gay joke. It was a fetish joke. Seriously, what about that coffee?"

Rook sighed. "You're killing me. You know I don't drink that dirt. What's going on?"

Tatum shifted his weight. "It was just north of your property here; thought I'd give you a heads up."

"What was just north?" Rook popped the refrigerator open to find him a drink: half-empty carton of eggs, applesauce, a near-depleted gallon of skim milk, iceberg lettuce, Coors Light, cottage cheese, mustard, an ancient container of Chinese he'd forgotten about, and orange juice. The orange juice was too precious. Tate would have to settle for beer or water.

Tatum was propped against the frame of the kitchen entryway. "You know those hikers who were missing? Well, one turned up."

Rook pulled his head out of the refrigerator. "One?" He pulled two glasses out of a cabinet over the sink.

"Mitchell Henderson. Twenty-three-year-old Caucasian male, five eleven, one hundred eighty pounds, blond hair, blue eyes . . ." He paused for a second. "And an organ donor."

Tatum had a knack for remembering things, usually trivial. Rook would've been surprised if he *hadn't* just recited everything from the missing guy's driver's license. He would've bet that Tatum knew the number as well as the issue and expiration date.

"I'm just gonna assume he's dead. How?"

"That's why I thought I'd come visit you. The guy was torn apart."

Rook thought about the mangled grouse. He finished filling the glasses with water and handed one to Tatum. "Wild animal?"

"It's hard to tell. Dr. Harper is doing a preliminary autopsy before we ship him up to Berryville. We're still canvassing the area looking for the rest." Tatum swallowed hard.

Rook sipped calmly on his water. "What do you mean 'the rest?'"

"Man, you don't even want to know. That poor guy was ripped apart. There's still some of him unaccounted for."

They both stared in silence for a moment. "I'm gonna stop playing twenty questions. I don't want to hear

19

anymore, but thanks for letting me know, Tate."

"Nuncaproblema, senor. I did it mostly for Tank." Tatum grinned. "How's my little buddy been?"

"Shriveled and unused?" Rook was proud of his quick remark.

"Harhar. I meant Tank, smartass."

"He's still outside. Make yourself useful and let him in."

Tatum complied and Tank flew through the doorway with a jumping kiss directed at him.

"Hey, hey, buddy. Why don't we get down?" He took Tank's paws off his stomach, which had left muddy prints all over his uniform.

Rook laughed. "Guess it rained last night."

Tatum tussled the fur on Tank's head and wiped at the mud. "I gotta go finish canvassing with the rest of the guys. Keep an eye out and be safe. My gut is telling me this is going to be messy."

Chapter 4

Rook's blue pickup bounced down the dirt road away from his cabin for about a mile before being fed onto a river of asphalt, known otherwise as Route 35, which weaved its way through boundless miles of forest. Kyruht was only fourteen miles away and was the closest, and friendliest, town in Rook's life. His body went on autopilot and his mind drifted through the trees whizzing by. Tank stood in the bed of the truck with his face to the oncoming wind, ears flapping. The pressure against his cheek flaps made it seem like he was smiling.

When a bump in the road jolted his mind back, he checked his hands at ten and two. He daydreamed, and was a "space cadet," as Carol had called him, but he prided himself on never mentally venturing so far as to be a peril to the world around him. He briefly thought about how nice it would have been to be a real space cadet, or astronaut, rather. He imagined floating through the quiet of space in some suit connected via umbilical to a ship, admiring the infinity of stars and cosmos, marveling at the earth and its magnificence from an external point of view. He also imagined Tank floating beside him in some doggy suit where his tail was free to wag.

His thoughts eventually wandered to the obsidian carving nestled in the cushion next to him on the pickup's bench seat. It bounced and swayed on its side with the movements of the truck. Keeping a cautious eye toward the road, he picked it up and examined it as he had before. The figurine retained its dark and ominous feeling, but wasn't quite as unsettling as it had been when he first found it. Granted, he wasn't being eyed by a hundred-pound Labrador this time.

Tank had given him grief when he saw the figurine get tossed into the truck. He first tried to jump into the passenger side and retrieve the statue. Rook supposed he meant to steal it and hide it. Stopped short by his leash, Tank resorted to one of his many faces. This one bordered between pathetic and concerned. Rook didn't fall for it and instead tossed him in the back, though Tank quickly forgot what was bothering him once the winds started flying by. There were important things to sniff.

Rook tossed the figurine into the glove box and glanced over his shoulder. The wolf figurine would have to wait in the truck for a couple of errands before he made it to Jon's pawnshop. Tank was moving excitedly back and forth, checking for any new scents on either side of the bed as the truck zipped down the road.

As he drew nearer to the town, the number of asphalt tributaries leading from homes to the main road increased until an area populated with several buildings came into view. The highway ran straight through the middle of town. On either side businesses served the small market. Distance Grocery served as a one-stop destination with fuel pumps out front. It was a small town's lifeblood and provided everything from groceries, clothing, and hunting and fishing supplies, to hardware, medicines, and stamps. The stamps were a point of contention with the town post office, which felt they should be the only pony with that trick.

Additionally there was Bender's Bar and Grill; Shelby's Diner, which served the best apple pie in the state; First Lutheran Church; the Kyruht all-in-one police station, morgue, and community center; Jon's pawn shop, the only one in the county; First National Bank of Kyruht, and a Dairy Queen. It was a small town prerequisite to contain a DQ. Just outside of the town center and off the main highway were the school, kindergarten through twelfth grade all-inclusive, the football field, and Beck's salvage yard, which was a veritable who's who of rusted Fords and Dodges.

When Rook pulled into town, he drove straight into the police station parking lot and parked. Tank knew exactly what was going on and paced anxiously in the bed of the truck as he waited for the tailgate to be opened. Once it was, he jumped out and padded to the front door of the station.

Rosalyn Redford was the receptionist, secretary, record keeper, and underpaid general operator of the Kyruht Police station.

"Morning, hun." She nodded to Rook as he and Tank walked by the front desk.

"Morning, Rose. How's George?"

"Stubborn as a mule, dumb as an ass, and the love of my life." She grinned. "He was up and about last night. Doctors said that, as they wean him off the pain meds, he'll be grumpy. I'd say that was an under-statement."

Rook chuckled with her and watched as she waddled around to a file cabinet. She was one of the largest women in Kyruht and one of the kindest. "So it's all right if I leave Tank here to play with Duke for a while right?" Duke was a German shepherd that wasn't an official K-9 unit, but gladly served the force both as mascot and intimidator. His doggie bed rested in an alcove across from one of the two jail cells.

"It's always all right."

"Good, because he already ran back there." Rook smiled. Tank hadn't stopped to greet Rose. He went straight through the open door to the holding area in the back. "You ever actually lock that door?" he asked.

"Why bother? Duke has it under control. You gonna be heading to the diner?" She smiled coyly.

"I might swing by for a bite after I hit Distance."

"Mmmm hmm." She stared at him from over her reading glasses. "Just gonna grab a piece of pie, hmm? Why don't you ask that young woman out? You stop by that diner every time you come to town, honey."

Rook evaded, "That's not why I go there, Rose. I just like to take the time to enjoy some real food."

"If you want real food, you should come over for dinner sometime. I make meatloaf that'll knock you on your ass. You can bring Dawn!"

"I'm NOT asking her out."

She sighed. "Have you put any thought into getting a job here in town? You'd get to see her more that way, you know."

"I'm still coasting all right on the inheritance for now."

"You never did tell me about your parents."

"Not something I talk about."

She stared at him, trying to pierce his resolve with fiery eyes, and placed a hand on her hip. He met her eyes stone-faced. It really was something he didn't discuss.

When he didn't respond, she moved on. "Hmm. Well, I'll set you up with a steady paycheck if the well starts to run dry before you write that bestseller. I'm not saying I could get you a job at the diner," she said, winking, "but I know Miles has been shorthanded over there at Distance."

"Thank you, Rose."

Both dogs barked loudly in the holding area.

"You got someone back there?"

"Just some drifter passing through that had a few too many. Sue had Bobby toss him in overnight to sober up before he took out anymore stop signs." Sue, or Sheriff Wzorek, as everyone but Rose referred to her, was a heavy-handed, yet just, agent of law enforcement in Kyruht. She had taken Tatum under her wing and he eagerly followed her like a puppy.

"You know anything about the body they found north of my place?"

Rose frowned. "Sue and Bobby are still up there canvassing the area with the few guys Berryville sent down to help." She called Tatum by his first name, Bobby. No one had a title around Rose. "It's so sad. I hope the other young man is all right, wherever he is. I don't remember the last time we had anything more than a missing yard flamingo or smashed stop signs."

The dogs barked angrily again. Rose stepped out from behind the desk area and walked to the holding area. Rook followed.

A large, unshaven man was leaning against the

bars of his cell, holding a red rubber ball. The dog's toy had rolled within his reach and he promptly snatched it up.

He spoke in a baby voice to Duke and Tank. "You want the ball? You want the ball?" His tone then altered significantly. "You'll get the damn ball when I get out of here." His statement seemed more directed at them now than the dogs.

"Now, Mr. Benedict, play nice. You know full well I don't have the authority to release you, but if you give the boys back their ball, I'll make sure Sue approves your release first thing when she gets back." Rose's voice was soft and gentle, yet commanding. She could've convinced the man to not only relinquish the ball, but also to take her out to dinner and a movie if she wanted. Rook quietly watched her work her magic. She smiled and waited for Benedict to oblige.

Benedict looked almost beastly with his thick stubble, broad shoulders, and heavy coat. He huffed and tossed the ball through the bars. "Fetch." He then returned to the bed in his cell and rested with his arms crossed behind his head.

Duke scooped the ball up on the second bounce while Tank missed entirely and skidded headfirst into the drywall. Rose turned with a pop in her step and a pleased grin and left the room. Rook turned to follow but stopped in his tracks when Benedict spoke with a condescending tone.

"Boy."

The man had hit directly on to one of Rook's nerves. He hated being called "boy" or "kid" or "sport" or any childlike name. After his adoptive parents had died, everyone talked down to him and treated him like a child, when in reality, the event had made him more of a man than his "father" ever was. His "father" wasn't even human. Rook bounced around foster homes as a "kid" for several years and then hit the road on his own as soon as he turned eighteen and finished high school.

He turned to face Benedict, who was still in his bed staring at the ceiling with his hands behind his head. He waited. Benedict spoke again without taking his eyes off the ceiling.

"The black veins. Do they burn yet?"

Rook scratched his chin. "What are you talking about?"

"C'mon, kiddo. Don't tell me you haven't noticed."

The "kiddo" made Rook tense his jaw. His fingers curled loosely into his palms.

"Aren't writers supposed to be observant?" He laughed. His voice seemed raspier and harsher than before. "Your arm, Rookie."

"Who are you? Why do you keep calling me . . ."

The man interrupted him, "This is going to be fun!" His eyes had not averted. He was still staring straight up in bed.

Rook stepped toward the cell and grasped the bars tightly. "What is your problem?"

Benedict sat up and stared at him. "What?"

"Why the hell were you talking like that? How'd you even know my name?"

The bear of a man stood and faced him. "I don't know what you're on, but I haven't said a word to you. You've been standing there talking to yourself."

"You called me 'boy' and asked about black veins."

"You know, there's another cell right over there. It's not padded, but I'm sure that the secretary up there could cover it with pillows for you." He chuckled and sounded like a grizzly bear grunting merrily.

Rook returned to the front of the building without another word and asked Rose about Benedict. She repeated to him that Arthur Benedict was just a drifter from up north who had a valid state ID, a shitty forest green Geo with fresh dents in the front bumper, and a couple thousand dollars cash on his person. She had no idea where he was from, where he was headed, or why he was walking around with wads of cash. She did confirm that he seemed to be living out of his car and asked Rook how he thought a man Benedict's size would live in a Geo.

Chapter 5

Leaving Tank at the station and his car parked in the lot, Rook walked across the street toward Distance. He thought about his conversation with Benedict and wondered what he had meant by black veins. Rolling up the sleeve of his hoodie, he examined his forearm. There was nothing unusual. The same scar stretched from his elbow a good three inches in the direction of his wrist and his skin was ghostly pale, but otherwise healthy, and the veins near the surface were a mostly obscured, light blue.

Rook then rolled down his sleeve and thought about what he was doing. He was letting a conversation with a drunkard get under his skin. Still, he was compelled to check the other arm. He'd never been one to let a curiosity slide.

When he rolled up his right sleeve, he found that the veins in that arm seemed different. Rather than a light blue, they were a dull gray, yet more visible with life flowing through them. It had to be a trick of the light. His mind was getting carried away.

It wasn't until a fast-approaching car horn sounded that Rook stopped staring at his arm. He had come to a stop, standing in the middle of the two-lane highway. The car swerved to the outside of the lane to avoid him, horn blaring all the way. He put a palm in the air and apologized to the driver who had momentarily slowed ahead of him. The red lights on the back of the car disappeared and the driver went on his way.

It was stupid to think some town drunk at the jail foresaw burning, black veins in Rook's arm. He dismissed the thought and the trick of the light and trotted to the other side of the street.

Distance Grocery started out as a small family business nearly a century before and had made the family very wealthy due to a monopoly of the market. They boasted twelve aisles and three registers. The whole place was packed with displays and stacks of products, and every inch of space on the walls had some sort of hanging fixture with more merchandise. And, if they didn't have what you were looking for, they'd order it at no extra expense. They'd "Go the Distance!"

Bells hanging from the doors jingled as Rook walked in.

"Hel... Never mind. It's just you." Mike was sitting on one of the checkout counters next to his register. "What's up, man?"

"Say it."

"Ah, c'mon." Mike protested and then proceeded, sarcastic and lackluster, "Welcome to Distance Grocery where we'll go the Distance for you! Ass."

"You love it." Rook grinned. "You and Barry the only ones working today?"

Barry nodded quietly from his spot leaning against the same counter. He and Mike had been talking when Rook walked in. Barry was a loner and reputably the only marijuana dealer in town. He never said much, his dark hair was disheveled and clothing tattered, and he always had a toothpick, pen cap, or cigarette in his mouth. He fit the burnout stereotype very well, even wearing a matching blue apron with Mike.

Mike, on the other hand, always wore the trendiest clothing, was a popular, strong-jawed, blond-haired, athletic cornerback at the school, followed the Ducks with a religious passion, and planned to attend Oregon University after graduation. In other words, he was the standard jock.

Mike and Barry had grown up together and were inseparable despite their differences. They did chase the same girls, which more often than not led to problems. Neither would get the girl, and instead, they'd end up smoking and getting wasted together at weekly bonfires.

"Just ask her out, man! You know she works the diner on Saturdays, not here." Mike didn't wait for a response and instead carried on, "If you do hit that, you gotta take pictures or something. Barry here has had the hots for her since we were freshmen and she was a senior. That's nearly a four-year-old set of blue balls!" Both teens laughed.

Rook let a chuckle escape before getting serious. "I wasn't asking about her."

"Riiiiiiiiight."

"I was asking about the boss man. Miles was supposed to have ordered a new battery for my laptop." Miles was to have, in fact, ordered a new battery, but Rook wouldn't have minded seeing Dawn. While the town seemed intent on meddling in his love life, he didn't care for the high school feel, and the usual town prodding wore thin after a while. He was a grown man and would go after her if he wanted to, but the idea of her, the fantasy, was much more exciting. He enjoyed her company for the visual stimulation and little affection she threw at him. It was a game and he was content as a humble pawn, though if the queen were to suddenly offer herself up to him, he wouldn't object.

Mike meanwhile kept his thoughts on Miles. "That little sow only works when he feels like it. He'll probably stroll in later."

"Problems again?"

"Just the same old shit. I'm gonna quit this place."

"And work where? Your options are kind of limited in this town."

"I don't know. Bender's, maybe? But I'm really quitting this time," Mike assured him.

Rook knew he wouldn't quit. "How many times have you said that?"

"Ah shaddup. You gonna buy something or not?"

"Light bulbs, milk, bread, orange juice, and a boat load of kibble."

"You know where it's all at." Mike wagged a finger in the direction of the aisles.

Mrs. Kuhrzman, a drama teacher at the school, was the only other person in the store. Even for mid-morning, it was slow. Rook was mulling over the vital decision between Fruity Os and Crunch when a blood-curdling scream echoed from a few aisles away.

Rook dropped the basket he had been filling and ran to the end of his aisle. As he rounded the end cap, Mike and Barry ran by. Mike reached Mrs. Kuhrzman's aisle first. When Rook and Barry arrived, Mike was doing an awkward, heavy-footed dance in front of her. She was standing with her spotted, leathery hands clutched tightly at her withered jowls and her mouth hung wide. What life still coursed through her had drained completely out of her face and Rook could tell she wasn't breathing. If it weren't for her black and white sweater with zebras on the border and long, fall-leaf-patterned skirt, she would've looked like Edvard Munch's silent screamer.

"Get it! Get it!" Mike commanded as he continued to stomp wildly.

"Get wha. . . . Holy shit, that thing is huge!" Rook's "what" blended right into the swearing when he saw what had terrified Mrs. Kuhrzman.

A plump, hairy, oversized wolf spider had scurried out from behind a box of penne when she moved it. It was dodging Mike's footfalls, despite its obesity, and frantically searched for an opening under the shelving it could squeeze in to.

Rook squelched his fear from the initial shock and placed a hand firmly on Mike's shoulder. "Stop, stop, stop. Don't kill it."

Mike was confused. Mrs. Kuhrzman was horrified by what Rook was about to do. Barry remained silent but observant.

The spider gave up trying to squeeze into hiding and backed into the thin, metal flap blocking her escape. She bunched four legs in front of herself defensively and left the other four spread for a potential dash. Through her six eyes she watched and waited for movement.

"You're not going to... OH!" Mrs. Kuhrzman fainted as Rook used his trained hand to quickly pluck the spider from its stance. Mike braced her and let her slide to a kind of crumpled, sitting position on the floor.

When he was a child, he spent as much time outside of the house as possible and became an expert in the fields of kickball, baseball, football, fence hopping, tree climbing, and bug catching. The trick was to quickly, but gently pin the arachnid between the thumb and pointer finger. Softly pinching between the thorax and abdomen, the spider had no way to bend and bite. Too much pressure, though, and internal organs would be crushed. Legs were also apt to be broken in the chaotic squirm that ensued.

Rook held the spider firm and examined it. She was indeed an oversized wolf spider and most likely had been more terrified than Mrs. Kuhrzman.

"You scared the shit out of us, Mrs. K." Mike tended to the fallen Kuhrzman.

Watching Rook and the spider with both wide-eyed terror and disgust from her spot on the floor, Mrs. K spoke, "How can you do *that*?! That hideous creature should have all its legs pulled out, be pinned to a rock, and have birds feasting on its innards for all eternity like the tortured Prometheus!"

Rook ignored her overdramatic rant and walked toward the front doors to release the critter before it injured itself.

"School's out, Mrs. K. I don't need to hear about any titans who pissed off the gods by giving man fire." Mike helped her to her feet.

Mrs. K let a pleased smile out at Mike's correct identification of Prometheus, sure that she must have been responsible for his knowledge. "So you were paying attention!"

"Nah. I just read that on the Internet." He grinned at her. "I still sleep in your class." He poked fun, even though he really had paid attention. Normally drama was boring, but when Mrs. K got off subject and went on one of her rants about Greek and Roman mythology it was entertaining.

She guffawed and patted any grime from the floor off her dress.

Chapter 6

Shelby's was an L-shaped 50s diner with a sky blue and steel chrome color scheme, homegrown waitresses, and a perpetual mixture of bacon, eggs, hash browns, cinnamon rolls, and pancakes that clung to the air.

Rook's favorite homegrown waitress from Kyruht was Dawn. Her long, brunette hair bounced on her slender frame as she approached him with a big smile. Her eyes were the same shade of blue as her uniform. The blouse had a button that was never clasped and the knee-length skirt was raised just a couple inches higher than the other waitresses. She wasn't a superficial girl, but she knew that working with what she'd been given would result in better tips.

"Hey, hot stuff! What can I get you?" A little flirting also increased tips exponentially.

Rook smiled and ordered, "Can I just get a croissant, some scrambled eggs and bacon, and a glass of orange juice?"

"Do you ever order anything different?" Dawn asked. She was twenty-one, four years younger than Rook. Instead of going to college immediately after high school, she worked two jobs.

"Hey, I occasionally get a cinnamon roll. Cut me some slack."

"How's the novel coming?"

"I'm starting a new one."

"Did you ever finish the last one?"

"Nope. I'll finish this one, though."

"You said that about the *last* one."

"I mean it this time," Rook assured her.

"I'll believe it when I see it." She grinned.

Rook leaned back in his booth seat and changed the subject with a tease. "So am I going to get my order placed today?"

"Oh hush." Dawn turned around with a fake pout and, with an exaggerated wiggle of her hips, left to place the order with the cook.

The exaggerated wiggle made Rook's blood pump faster. Seeing her shapely backside deliberately used to taunt made his pants tighten involuntarily. Luckily he was hidden under the tabletop. Countless times books, jackets, and counter tops saved him and every other man in existence from embarrassment.

As he sat thinking about the complex relationship between mankind and its better half, Dawn promptly returned with his orange juice and started in with some not-so-small talk. He expected inquiries about the weather and updates on how the Woodsmen had done in the previous Friday night's football game, but today was different.

"Did you hear about the hiker they found outside of town?!" She spoke with an unusual mix of excitement and genuine concern. He could tell she was really worried but at the same time trying to maintain her routine waitress banter and attitude.

"Yeah. Officer Tatum swung by this morning to tell me about it." He swigged some of the tangy, sweet orange juice and looked at her eyes, the eyes torn out in his nightmare.

"My cousin, who lives down Route 35, just texted that she saw the ambulance on its way back! I imagine it'll be here shortly." She leaned against the table with one delicate hand and placed the other on her hip.

The fascination with the dead driving in was juxtaposed by the fact that even out in a deep forest community, technology had slithered its way in and texting was now the way for small town gossip to travel. He would be one to judge, though. He had longed for and attained the isolation of such a town, but brought television, Internet, video gaming, and the like into his humble cabin.

"It is a shame, a terrible tragedy. I'm sure they'll catch whatever animal did that. I just hope the other hiker fared better." Rook really did recognize the horror that the death was, but he couldn't help but let his thoughts wander and consider the difference between a death in a community like Kyruht versus a death in a big city. People die by the score daily in big cities and get no more than thirty seconds in the nightly news. In Kyruht it would be the talk of the town for a month, if not longer. What made a month better than thirty seconds, though? Forgetting was forgetting. People should never be forgotten. Monsters should.

Dawn shifted her weight from one hip to the other while keeping her hand on the table. Her hands showed no sign of age. They were smooth and without blemish. There were no scars or protruding veins or even a hangnail. She was physically perfect down to the cuticle.

She stared at him in thought for a moment, watching the wheels turn. Finally she sat down across from him. "Something's different about you today."

It was true. He wasn't doting attention on her as he normally would. "Sorry. I get introspective and thoughtful when I've had an odd day, and believe me, it's been an odd twenty-four hours."

That was also true.

"What has the gossip mill got on that Benedict guy locked up at the station?"

Dawn sat up straight and leaned forward; gossip physically perked her up. Though Rook envisioned she was already plenty perky. "Not a whole lot yet. Although Mr. Renelette thinks he's a Russian spy sent to gather intel on us."

She laughed and Rook followed suit. Renelette was an extremely interesting, overall-clad gray beard, who, while having many genuine stories, was known for his conspiracy theories. He was a diner faithful, and every morning, at eight o'clock sharp, would have his newspaper and coffee in the corner booth, keeping a watchful eye on the highway and every patron dining through. Once, Rook spent an hour listening to him talking about World War II in Japan, concubines, jewelry heists, backroom dealing, the steel industry, and drug dealers at a Village Inn in Omaha that he used to frequent. He was undoubtedly captivating, and a treasure trove of knowledge and stories, but you never knew truth from fiction. He was of a dying breed of oral storytellers that intertwined history and myth so well he could get you believing Hitler once danced polka with Sasquatch.

Dawn continued and derailed Rook's conductor-less train of thought. "I do know that they found him out around the junkyard. He took out a school zone sign and was stumbling back and forth trying to replant the sign . . . in the pavement."

Benedict seemed a normal drunk by all appearances, a man lost and drifting through life or maybe running from something, but he had no record, no black sheet, and no prophesies of dark veins and end of times to preach around town. Not that anyone else had heard anyway. Rook imagined him roaring into town on a chariot drawn by steeds black as midnight, broad chest robed in darkness, cackling madly, yelling to the townsfolk that they would all burn with black veins. His imagination *really was* in overdrive.

All the introspection and contemplative thought was boring and pretentious around others. He needed to snap out of it and bottle up the creative thinking until he got home in front of his laptop. Thankfully the silent ambulance rolled up to the station right on cue and spared Dawn from anymore of his flavorless conversation. He figured she was thankful anyway. He would be if he had to talk to himself.

They could see the ambulance across the street through the diner's wall-to-wall windows. It pulled into the parking lot, past Benedict's forest green Geo, and went around behind the building. There was a loading bay where they could take corpses into the morgue discreetly, if it weren't for the fact that the rear of the station was perpendicular to the bisecting highway.

The EMTs backed the ambulance up to the doors as close as possible. The EMT on the passenger side was a young, blond woman who would have been beautiful if not for the pallid complexion and dark circles under her tired eyes. Her hair bounced in a ponytail draped on her navy blue shoulder as she swiftly moved to the rear and opened the cargo doors. The driver was a portly man just a shade under average height. He had narrow shoulders and a belly that reached out as far as his arms. He flicked a cigarette into a puddle as he stepped out of the ambulance. After a scratch through his brown hair, he tugged at his pants and sauntered behind the far side of the vehicle.

The woman already had the black-bag-laden gurney rolling out by the time the driver got around. She hoisted the gurney over the lip of the pavement leading into the double doors. There was the better part of a full-grown man bagged on the gurney but she maneu-vered it effortlessly with her tiny but athletic build. Rook guessed she was a runner. The runner and the rotund one disappeared inside.

Rose had given him a full tour of the station once before. The body bag would be wheeled down a dirty, yellow-walled hallway toward the heavily locked door that provided rear entrance to the holding cells. Off to the right was the autopsy room where Dr. Harper would do his work. The remains would be carefully lifted onto a cold, steel slab and, once the doctor removed them from the bag, arranged as closely resembling a normal body as possible. It was gruesome work, but they needed to assemble an idea of what happened before they shipped the body off to Berryville for better examination.

He dismissed the morbid thoughts and wolfed down his late breakfast when Dawn brought it to him. He got a quick "Thank you" in before his hands shoved a fork full of eggs down the hatch. They were fluffy and heavily peppered, just the way he liked them. Dawn took care of some other customers while he masticated like swine.

When she returned to clear Rook's nearly spotless plates, she obligatorily asked if he wanted anything more, even though she knew the answer. He was a creature of routine. She then slid the bill on the table in its little black book and told him she was going on a smoke break in a few minutes if he wanted to join her. He briefly considered the possibility that her offer was just a nicety in order to acquire a better tip. He quickly decided that, either way, he'd be happy to go chat with her outside the diner. She took his payment to the register, checked on her tables, and, without a word about the tip, walked outside with him. On the way they exchanged pleasantries about each other's plans for the evening and the storm that forecasters thought was brewing.

There was a chill in the air outside. Winter taunted them with cold breezes to assure them it was coming. Snug in his hoodie, he watched her slide on her coat and pull out a pack of cigarettes and a lighter. She popped one in her mouth and rolled the flint to spark, cupping her hand around the procedure. Watching her engage in the nasty habit should've lost her points in his eyes, but he didn't seem to care. It added to her not-good-for-me-so-I-want-it appeal if anything. Given the opportunity, he'd still kiss her, though he might offer up a mint. She walked a fine line between a woman he wanted and a woman he wanted to avoid. It was that tightrope walk that kept him from ever really pursuing her, but he'd watch the show.

She breathed in the toxic fumes and then exhaled with a nod over toward Distance. "Hey, guys!"

Mike and Barry were smoking behind the store, though Rook had a hunch what they had rolled up wasn't tobacco. They smiled ear-to-ear and trotted over, Mike coughing up smoke as he crossed.

"What's up?" Mike asked on behalf of Barry and himself.

Dawn replied, "Not much. Just chit chatting with Rook."

Barry and Mike both flashed him a grin.

"Who's watching the store?" Rook asked them. "I thought you were the only two working."

"One of Miles's new hires came in for training."

"So you left the entire store in the hands of a newbie who just started today and knows absolutely nothing about the job?"

"Well, when you say it like that, you make us sound irresponsible. Is something the matter, Rook? Do you not want us out here?" Mike teased.

Dawn giggled.

"Harhar." Rook leaned back against the diner.

"Are you guys gonna go to homecoming?" Dawn asked the boys.

"Why yes. Barry is being antisocial, but I'll be attending." Mike bent halfway in what he must have imagined was an old-time, chivalrous bow. It more resembled a kowtow, a Japanese sign of respect, but not the one he was looking for. "Would you care to be my arm candy?"

He had balls. *You have to give him credit for that,* Rook thought to himself.

Barry kicked at the gravel, never making eye contact with Dawn but artfully stealing looks.

"That ship sailed a long time ago, hun. I'm too old for that stuff. You should take one of the girls in your class," she politely declined.

Mike almost visibly cringed. It was as if a knife labeled "Friend Zone" had been slipped in under his rib cage.

Barry held back a snicker.

"I got a dozen different girls at the school I can take," Mike gloated and reassured himself.

"Oooh, a dozen, and at such a small school! I bet at least one of them is your cousin!" Dawn laid down a playful zinger.

"Second cousin, so she's legal," he joked.

They all laughed at the let's-make-people-uncomfor-table style of humor.

Mike handed what he was smoking to Barry, who promptly puffed, and then he steered the conversation. "So what do you think happened with those hikers?"

"Sounds like it may have been a bear, or a pack of wolves," Rook chimed in.

"You think they dragged away the other guy?"

Before Rook could hypothesize, Dawn jumped in.

"Let's not talk about that. It's gross enough without brooding over it."

"Brooding?" Rook and Mike both repeated.

"Yeah, it means preoccupied with something morbid."

Mike responded first. "Well, we know that. It's just that . . ." He stopped himself.

Rook held his tongue.

"You were gonna say you didn't think I knew a word like that! You dick!" She punched him in the shoulder. Her tiny fist landed square, but didn't faze him in the least. He rolled his shoulder back with the blow and laughed. He was probably glad to have been touched by her. She glared at Rook, too.

"Hey, don't look at me like that. I was just going to say nice word!" He chuckled, but then conceded to her scowl. "All right, fine." He turned his shoulder so she could tap him one.

After her second slug of the day, she took another drag on her cigarette and, after one last pout, she cracked a smile. She looked at Barry. "I like you. You don't talk."

Barry, who normally maintained his mysteriously confident appearance, blushed noticeably.

A young girl who looked like she was from their high school popped her head out from Distance's back door. She saw the boys and then stepped out. She was even smaller than Dawn and had frizzy, brown hair falling out of a ponytail. In her hair and on her shoulder and chest was what appeared to be chunky pasta sauce. She looked as if she was about to cry.

Mike looked over at her. "Ah, jeez. What did she do?" He directed his inquiry toward Barry. Then he turned his attention to Rook and Dawn. "Gotta go, guys. See ya!"

Chapter 7

Jon's shop was packed to the brim with goods when Rook stepped in and the doorbells jingled overhead. There were the usual speakers, jewelry, instruments, and weaponry found in every pawnshop and then there were the unusual items. Jon doubled his store as a place of heritage, though it was heritage off of which he wasn't too proud to make a buck.

He had stock of Native American hand drums that children would spin to make the little balls at either end of a string strike a repetitive tapping noise and irritate their parents, as well as several ornate wooden carvings, many of which he had done himself. He pandered to the white man's need to see beads and feathers but peppered in some true cultural artifacts. He proudly displayed a tomahawk that had belonged to his grandfather, as well as a peace pipe, in a glass case near contemporary gear passing hunters had sold.

Behind the counter were several black and white pictures. One in particular struck Rook the first time he saw it. It was a picture of a stoic Shasta Indian forefather sitting stiffly upright in a chair dressed in traditional dried hides. Still a relatively young man in the picture, he had long black hair and leathery skin with tribal paint on the same strong cheeks shared by Jon, except one of those cheeks was scarred. His eyes stared somewhere behind the camera and propped up against his chair was a rifle, a prized possession no doubt. In one hand resting on his thigh, the man held a bone tomahawk with small feathers laced to the top. The scene-stealer, though, was perched on the man's other arm, held horizontally at his side. A large raven, as Jon had later informed him, rested just as stoically with its talons wrapped around the leather brace on his arm. Attached to one of its feet was another small strip of leather, used both to identify the bird and tether it when necessary. Hunters through and through, Jon had said.

When Rook asked why it wasn't a hawk or falcon, Jon explained that his grandfather hadn't deliberately chosen the raven; it found him and became a valuable asset on hunts. When he was a boy, Jon's grandfather told him the story of his friendship with the animal.

He and the other men of the tribe had been trailing an elk for hours. They stepped lightly through the woods, following the broken branches and excrement the elk left behind. Every time it seemed they were closing in, the elk pulled them farther away. He was still very young at the time and, being the youngest and most inexperienced among the hunters, he fatigued faster. When they crossed a stream, he stopped to drink some water and, in doing so, let them get farther ahead. With his head down and palms on the pebbles, he took deep drinks of the cool stream. It was when he was distracted by the water that a wolf approached him. He heard the snarling too late. The wolf was rabid and hunting on his own, desperate enough for food that it attacked a man. The wolf leapt on him before he could gain his feet and went straight for his neck. He punched it in the muzzle but didn't completely avoid the bite. It tore his cheek open and left it hanging in a mangled flap. The wolf redirected its attention to the hand that had hit it and bit down hard, tearing the flesh with ease. Its claws tore at him as the wolf struggled to keep him down and maintain its bite. As he screamed for help, a large raven swooped down from the heavens and clawed at the wolf's eyes, quickly blinding it. The wolf wailed in pain and Jon's grandfather seized the opportunity to grab his tomahawk. He ended the beast's suffering as quickly and mercifully as he could, despite its vicious attack.

His fellow hunters had heard his cries and returned to find him badly wounded and slumped over the wolf. The raven watched quietly from the branches above as they lifted him to his feet and carried him, and the carcass, back to the village.

It was soon evident that he had contracted disease from the wolf, but his mother, who was the tribe's healer, watched over him night after night as he cried in pain and his skin crawled. He would've scratched until he bled if they didn't restrain him. He would sweat his way in and out of consciousness, freezing with fever on a brush mat in their cedar dwelling. His mother chanted softly when she would hold him and treated him both with smoke and vile herbal mixes. After twenty days and nineteen nights of the torment, the disease left him. He had been chosen to survive. When he finally awoke from his last fever-induced sleep and gained strength, he climbed out to find that his mother hadn't been the only one watching over him. High in the branches of a nearby tree sat the raven. His people told him that it circled and stayed near them the entire time he was fighting for his life.

Days and weeks passed with the raven always overhead. It stayed near him even when they hunted and only strayed when it needed to hunt for itself. One evening, after a successful hunt, Jon's grandfather coaxed the bird from the trees with roasted elk meat. While the bird ate, he gently attached the leather lead that he could tether it with. The bird offered no resistance and, requiring little instruction, rapidly became a well-trained tool of the hunt. The Great Creator had forged a bond of the spirit between him and the animal; they were inseparable. He fashioned a tall cedar perch, which he placed outside his hut for the bird. It stayed there in the evenings and followed him in the day. The tether proved unnecessary, though he left the leather strip in place. For years the raven hunted with them and helped provide sustenance for the people until one morning, not long after the photograph, it disappeared from its perch and was never seen again.

The raven, Rook learned, was in many Native American stories. In some it was known as Creator, dropping the seed of life from his beak, allowing the world to emerge and bloom. In another story it was a matchmaker, coaxing early man from giant clams and then, after growing bored with man, freeing women from a chiton. That raven was so entertained and enamored by their paring that he became a protector of the bond between a man and a woman. Another fabled raven was a trickster who made a greedy seagull open the gift the Great Creator had given him, freeing the sun, moon, and stars.

When asked which raven he thought had come to his grandfather, Jon told him the story of the regretful Chief Raven. In Shasta folklore the raven was a symbol of both life and death. The raven flew between the worlds of the living and the dead, marked those to be given passage, and ultimately escorted travelers from one plane of existence to the next.

Chief Raven was granted the power to decide if humans and animals would have one life, or two, but Chief Raven, who enjoyed eating the eyes of carrion, was greedy and decreed that they should only have one life. Shortly after his decree, death found Chief Raven's family. After losing his children, he learned the error of his ways, but it was too late. He flew between the worlds, searching for a way to bring them back. Forever searching and following death, he allowed other regretful spirits with unfinished business to fly with him, promising to thwart evil like that which destroyed his family.

The wolf that had attacked his grandfather had been soured by evil, so the raven, recognizing a noble spirit of his own people, protected him. Weary from him his ceaseless journey, the raven stayed with his grandfather long after he had healed. When the time came for him to resume his search, he left, knowing that one day they would meet again in the world between worlds.

Rook hoped that Jon had a similarly informative and interesting story about the obsidian wolf he had found. His hand cupped the wolf in his hoodie. "Hey, Jon! You back there?"

The cluttered store was void of patrons and, seemingly, staff. It was empty behind the counter, though a thin haze of smoke drifting from the back room indicated someone was present. Incense clung to the air, but the smoke was something different.

Rook shouted through the smoke, "How do you even get away with that?"

"Hey, it's medicinal. There's nothing better to ease and clear the mind than glaucoma medicine." Jon stepped out from the back room.

"I have never seen your eyes look clouded by glaucoma."

"Then it's working." Jon grinned a toothy smile. He was an older man by Rook's standards, a kindly semi-centurion in his late fifties, though Rook was a quarter century himself. Jon was a Native American through and through and looked almost identical to his grand-father on the wall when he was serious, although that was rare. The one thing that really set him apart was the white feather he wore in his long, black hair at all times. Rook had never asked about it. He assumed it either had to do with heritage or sales.

"So, how is Tank?"

Everybody in the town seemed to look forward to Tank's visits more than Rook's. "He's doing just fine. He's over at the station playing with Duke right now."

Jon bent over and reached into a locked, lower, out-of-sight region of some glass shelves. "He's a mighty good dog. Give him a pat on the head for me. Ah, here it is." He withdrew a striking, silver lighter and tossed it to Rook. "Feel the weight of that sucker, eh?"

The lighter was indeed heavy in his hand. The reservoir and flint-striking mechanism were encased in real silver with a design inlay. The design illustrated a bow hunter among hemlocks with an elk in a three-scene display before, during, and after a kill wrapped all the way around the lighter. "Pretty cool."

"And I'll sell it to you at the discounted price of five hundred dollars."

"Five hundred dollars?! Some discount, Jon. You gonna sell me a hundred dollar pair of socks while you're being so generous?"

"That piece is easily worth a thousand. I'm taking a hit selling it to you so cheap. You know it would look great with that jade pocket knife of yours." He nodded to the lighter. "It's actually useful, too. Just imagine setting flame to some tinder in the fire pit you got out back."

"How much did you buy it for, Jon?"

He didn't miss a beat. "It doesn't matter how much I got it for. You can get it for an amazing price!"

"How much?" Rook insisted.

Jon sighed. "All right, I bought it off the guy for fifty bucks. I may have lied and told him it was a fake cast out of pewter. It's really silver, though."

"You really are a master of your craft, you know that?" They both laughed. "That actually brings me to why I'm here. Can you look at something for me?"

"Depends. Am I going to make money?"

"Not a penny." They both laughed again. Rook, still holding the lighter in one hand, pulled the obsidian carving out with the other and set it on the glass counter top. When he moved his hand away, giving Jon a clear view, he was baffled by the response.

"Get out of here right now! Take that *thing* with you!" Jon emphasized the word "thing" like it was an armed nuclear device.

"What? What's wrong, Jon? What did I do?"

"Take *it* and go now!" He waved his hands at Rook from behind the counter and backed away.

Dumbfounded, Rook stammered, "What the hell, Jon?"

"GET OUT!"

Rook grabbed the carving and spun toward the door. He could hear Jon mumbling a language he didn't understand and then the words "Not here" over his shoulder.

Chapter 8

Rook stumbled back to Shelby's, bewildered by Jon's behavior. He saw Mr. Renelette watching him through the window.

"Do you ever go anywhere, old man?" Rook said through the glass, not loud enough to be heard. A blip of anger had popped up in him in light of Jon's actions. He quickly felt ashamed for scolding Mr. Renelette through the glass. Mr. Renelette just stared.

Inside the diner Dawn was still hard at work. She was ever-so bent over a table, walking through the menu with a customer dressed in a flannel shirt and trucker's hat. She had two buttons undone on her blouse, just enough to tease and excite the customer into a gracious mood.

He quietly slipped into a booth before she noticed him and left her customer to decide what lunch would be best to ogle her over.

"What brings you back here twice in one day, hmm?" She grinned.

"Aside from the service?" he flirted. "Just felt like a drink all of a sudden." He really just wanted someone to talk to while he wrapped his head around Jon.

"A drink? You do realize this isn't exactly the place for booze, right?"

"You go straight to booze, huh? What if I meant a drink of orange juice?" he teased.

"You and that juice. I'm gonna go smoke quick while my table is getting situated. You want to join me?"

"Again? You and those smokes. Sure, why not?"

Once outside, she didn't waste any time beating

around the bush. "So what really brings you in? I can tell something is on your mind. You get this look on your face when you get off somewhere in thought. You did it this morning, too."

She pulled out a cigarette and her lighter while she spoke. The flint sparked, but the lighter didn't catch.

"Piece of shit. I just got it. That's what I get for buying it at Miles's store."

He still had the lighter Jon had been showing him. When Jon rushed him out, he had dropped it into his pocket and forgotten about it. "Here. Use this one."

She took the lighter from his hand. Through her cigarette she mumbled, "This is a nice lighter."

"Keep it." He played cool. "It's a gift from me to you." He would reimburse Jon for it later.

"I can't do that. This is too nice, Rook." She studied the engraved artwork carefully. "Hell, it's got a short film on it."

"Keep it. I insist. It's not every day I get to give a pretty girl a gift."

She laughed. He had laid it on too thick.

"Well, thank you. That was cute."

He backtracked to teasing. "Now don't think this means I support your smoking. Kissing a girl who smokes is like kissing an ashtray."

A mischievous smile spread across her face. "Is it now?" She stepped toward him. "Kissed a lot of smokin' girls, have you?" She was within a foot of him, looking directly into his eyes.

Surely she wasn't doing what he thought she was doing. He barely talked to her outside the diner and they'd never really hung out. He had assumed the invitations to join her on break had been nothing more than friendly gestures. Maybe they were more than friendly.

No. No, he was misreading the situation. He had to be. He was a quiet but friendly guy who had never shown her real interest or really pursued her. He'd made it clear he just enjoyed her company like all her other patrons.

Then there was the chance that she was simply being free-spirited. Dawn was the type to do what she wanted when she wanted. She was impulsive, and that's why her current beau had captured her attention. He was a legitimate biker in a real gang. It could've been Hell's Angels or Heaven's Demons or Corner-Drug-Store's Kittens. Rook hadn't cared enough to listen about the beau. He quickly pigeonholed him as a "bad-boy" and moved on.

Though the biker beau had her attention, she would never use the "B" word: "Boyfriend." The biker was in and out, off and on, which was inconsistent for someone who craved spontaneity. She wasn't a slut. She was a perpetual player picking a "bad boy" to sew wild oats once in a while, never settling on a townie. She was a "bad girl" with a sweet enough edge that everyone loved her, and here she was, standing within range of a kiss.

If only she knew the thought processes she sent men into, he thought, the amount of analysis he just did simply because she moved closer.

Sensing his hesitation, she spoke, but held her ground. "So do you think I'd taste like an ashtray?" She cocked her head and grinned. In her blue eyes he could see she was testing him, to see if he'd really go for it.

From deep within him a primal urge took hold. The urge was not one of sexual desire, but one of power and dominance. The unusual anger Jon had sparked was refocused into this new feeling, an absolute need to overcome cowardice. A voice from inside yelled at him to "*Fucking do it! Don't run from the bitch!*" It didn't feel like his normal inner voice. Something was different. He thought of the tentacle creature he dreamed of the previous evening.

To both Dawn's surprise and his own, he did it. He first raised his hand and brushed her hair over her right ear. His hand felt detached, acting of its own volition. He watched the brush of the hair while a confused expression furrowed Dawn's face. Then, forcefully, his hand grabbed the back of her neck and pulled her the rest of the way in. Their lips met, and after the initial contact, he gently bit her bottom lip. He slid his tongue in and it danced with hers. He felt her resist for a fraction of a second, but his hand held firm. She gave in to the moment and softly massaged his tongue with hers, but did not enter his mouth. She was the one being reserved. Her mouth was smoky, but on her, it seemed exotic and matched her fiery personality.

His other hand, which had been resting on her hip, started to explore the small of her back and then traced lower to her firm buttocks.

She broke away.

"I . . . I'm sorry. I don't know what just happened. I didn't mean to steal that kiss." He stuttered his words and backed up.

She took a deep swig of the cigarette she still held in her hand, studied him, exhaled, and smiled. "It's all right. Keep it. I insist. It's not every day I get to give a nice guy a kiss." She winked.

He let out a small laugh that was more like a sigh of relief. "Thank you. I uh . . . I got to get going." He prepared to run.

"Inspired to do some writing?" Her smile was nearly crippling; it was so beautiful and mischievous at the same time.

He laughed again and scratched at the back of his neck. "Yeah. Actually I am." He paused and selected careful words. "It's been an interesting day."

"I'll see you around, Rook."

And she would.

Chapter 9

The Ticians were a race of tall, skinny aborigines with giant heads that lived in the jungle and prided themselves on their argumentative skills. They had shouting matches that would echo through the jungle, louder even than howler monkeys. Unfortunately they would spend so much time arguing that they rarely accomplished anything. Rather than hunt, fish, or forage, they would argue for days on end about the most trivial things. They survived by talking the tribes of neighboring races into giving them a certain amount of their earned resources in exchange for empty promises. It was actually a rite of passage for a Tician man to negotiate one of the neighboring tribes out of their resources. The more they talked out of the neighboring races, the higher their status was within their own tribe.

Rook laughed out loud to himself as the Tician people unfolded onto the otherwise blank screen in front of him. He was quickly replacing the blinding white with paragraph after paragraph. The satire that was flowing out of him was good, and what's more, it was *flowing*. He hadn't had a good session at the keys in a while. His odd experiences during the past couple days had sparked creativity in him and he'd be damned if he didn't make use of it. Thoughts of Dawn frequented him, but he pushed them aside for the time being.

The Ticians were a small part of a fantasy world that was exploding into his mind. The jungle, a mountain range, sweeping plains of grassland, a quaint village, a vast, highly advanced city of engineering, a whole world was fitting together like puzzle pieces in his head. It wasn't the horror story he wanted to write, but it grabbed him by the ears and pulled him in.

The Gormads came to him next. They would be a husky, rotund people who were highly critical of everything. They would analyze the hair on a tick's ass and give thirty reasons why it wasn't good enough. While they would be a friendly people, who were wealthy from the fine products they exported, even though their production time was highly inefficient due to excessive scrutiny, they would be disliked by all the other races for the backhanded compliments they offered when they weren't telling you your first born child was two inches too short and looked more dimwitted than a cross-eyed cow.

The phone rang.

Rook was well into the story and didn't register the phone until it had rung four times. Whoever it was would have to wait. He wouldn't be torn away from the high that flow offered. His fingers waltzed through the alphabet without hesitation. His mind was spilling out into a magical land and he wanted to stay with it. If the phone call was important, the caller could leave a message on his answering machine. He was a firm believer in cell phones and voice mail, but out in the cabin, a cellular device wasn't always reliable, so he relented and got a landline.

It wasn't until Jon's voice interrupted the Gormads that he snapped out of his new world.

"Hey, Rook. It's Jon. I wanted to apologize for rushing you out of the store earlier. You caught me off guard with that thing." He paused and cleared his throat. "You should bring it over to my place this weekend and we'll talk. I believe you have a very significant piece there. Give me a call."

That thing . . .

His fingers stopped as he thought about the wolf. His stomach growled angrily and took precedence.

"Tank, I think I've been derailed for the night." He turned to the furry, brown Tank who was deep into licking himself. "Well, that's appetizing."

*

Rook couldn't remember when he had fallen asleep, as was often the case, but he knew where he was. The library was dark and empty again. His characters had all disappeared. The being he had seen the previous night was still there. He could feel it. The tentacle creature contaminated the room. The air was heavy with dust, as if the creature had stirred up several inches and spread it through the library like pestilence. It was easy to discern what books had been brushed off. The creature was still in back by a section meant to be forgotten.

He would've gotten rid of the books, but he could never completely erase the memories they contained. As much as he tried to cleanse his mind of those pages, they wouldn't disappear or be destroyed. So he carefully isolated them and left them to collect dust.

He walked toward the back, footsteps echoing through the aisles. No sign of the creature. Complete silence, and yet there was an energy primed to burst. Whatever the creature was, it was powerful and had an aura that encompassed the entire library, his entire mind.

Suddenly he felt compelled to venture deep into the depths of the library, into a part of his mind he had locked up. Beyond the dark bookshelves of pages never to be opened was a door. A dull gray, steel door surrounded by dirty, red brick, it was the most horrifying door he had ever seen and it was straight from his childhood. In his childhood, when the small, silver lock dangling on the latch was unhooked, it meant the fat man was waiting inside. In his mind he had welded the latch and changed the lock. His was a large, green lock similar to the one he had used in high school. It would never be open again as long as he could help it. Still, the words "Open it" whispered in his ear.

He reached his hand to the door and wrapped his fingers around the lock. The cold metal was welcome against his warm, sweaty palms, but he didn't want to open the door. No part of him really wanted to go through the door. It was as if an unseen hand was at his back, pushing him forward.

The fat man, the most revolting and nearly the most terrifying man he had ever known, was sealed beyond the door. He couldn't face that again. His hand dropped from the lock and he staggered backwards. As he exhaled deeply, the voice belonging to the tentacle creature boomed through the library.

"You were supposed to OPEN IT you coward!" it demanded. The voice, as it had been the previous night, was oddly familiar to Rook. It wasn't quite right, but he knew it from somewhere.

"No," Rook stated, bluntly objecting to the unseen force at work.

The voice demanded once more, "What did that fat fuck do to you?! Why is he locked away where I can't get to him?!"

Rook remained silent and steadfast. The twisted half smile he'd seen before flashed in front of his eyes again.

"You *will* let me in completely. Fight it all you want, but I will know and control every part of you," the voice hissed. "Now run along and play, kiddo . . ."

The voice trailed and disappeared. The aura of energy he had felt subsided, and the air cleared.

He slept.

*

When Rook awoke, Tank was either still deep into himself, or just started again. The chocolate hound stared at him as if he had just interrupted a sacred ritual. He could tell it was still dark outside, but he felt as if he had slept for hours. He looked at his alarm clock and hoped to God that Tank wasn't on the same session because eight hours had passed. Sunlight would be appearing soon. He had slept through the night in what seemed like the blink of an eye. He remembered a voice, and then the door.

"Have a nice vacation down there?" he asked Tank.

The lab took the vocalization as a sign his presence was requested and raised himself to all fours. He trotted over to the bedside. Rook was prepared to dodge any kisses after what he had witnessed, but Tank stopped short of delivery on his own. Instead, he took two cautious steps back.

"What's wrong?" Rook asked.

Tank stared at him like he was a stranger, then he growled.

"It's me, bud. Come here." He patted his thighs.

Tank remained at a distance.

"Fine. Be a grouch. I gotta piss anyway." Releasing a morning grunt as he lifted himself to his feet, Rook rolled his shoulders and stretched his arms over his head as he shuffled to the bathroom. The first time he passed the mirror he didn't notice. He stood at the toilet to relieve himself and scratched his head. It was when he was back in front of the mirror to wash his hands that he realized what freaked Tank out. His hands stopped, cold and motionless, the lukewarm water splashing in the basin. His mouth was twisted in a smile he didn't consciously make. His eyes were jet black.

"What the fuck?!" he cursed loudly to himself and flung the mirror open. Just medicine bottles. He closed his eyes and rubbed them vigorously. It was a trick of the light, a shimmer of hallucination; the whites of his eyes weren't black. They couldn't be. Slowly he shut the cabinet mirror to see his disheveled face. His hair was a mess and he needed to shave, but the smile was gone and his eyes were normal, aside from a few sleep goobers crystallized at the tear duct. He rubbed those out the rest of the way and his eyes remained normal. They were the eyes he had inherited from the devil himself, a reminder of his biological "father" he wished he didn't have, though he told himself his eyes were much softer and certainly kinder than those of his "father." There was no kindness in those, just evil.

Thankfully he didn't have to see his eyes or those of anyone he didn't care for anymore. Hearing the click of Tank's paws on the bathroom tile, he glanced over to see the dog halfway in the doorway, head cocked as if to say, "Where have *you* been?" His tail was wagging.

Confused but relieved, Rook crouched and patted Tank on the head. "If you can tell me what that just was, I will get you a gold-plated dog bowl and all the sirloin you can eat."

Tank slapped his cheek with his big, pink tongue.

"I just got dog crotch all over my face, didn't I?" Rook grimaced and wiped the saliva off his cheek. He released the hound and turned on the shower. "I needed a shower to wash off the heebie-jeebies anyway. Do that again, though, and I'll have a vet neuter you faster than you can say castration."

Chapter 10

"I don't know, man. I feel like Matthew McConaughey. I got ten years on some of these girls," Rook objected. He had been goaded into coming to Mike and Barry's pre-homecoming party against his better judgment. It was childish to give in when they called him a chicken. He could have easily hung up the phone, but here he was, showcasing his testicular fortitude because they had questioned his manhood. It was an everyman fault, the need to prove one's masculinity.

"I just keep getting older, but they stay the same age. All right, all right," Mike mimicked McConaughey's infamous line with the perfect amount of pacing and sinisterly smooth draw.

Rook couldn't resist laughing with him and Barry.

Barry passed a joint to Mike, who took a deep hit and exhaled. The party wasn't big, but twenty minors drinking and smoking at the shore didn't bode well for the one legal adult there.

The glowing bonfire burned through a bracing log and crumbled a little as Mike passed the joint back to Barry. "*Dazed and Confused*, man. That's an awesome movie." He stopped to wave to a pretty blond who was just approaching the bonfire with two other friends.

"Twenty-three minors," Rook kept count.

Mike continued where he was going, "Seriously, man. You're the older, mysterious guy to these girls. You could say you're a college guy!" He got excited as he arrived at the idea. "It'd be like shooting fish in a barrel."

"It'd be more like netting felonious minnows. They're jailbait, Mike."

"Not all of them. Just the majority." He handed Rook

a beer. "Relax and unwind, my friend. You're a good guy, easy to hang out with, but your ass is tighter than Ellen's over there." He pointed to the blond on the other side of the fire talking with her friends. More alcohol had magically manifested in their hands. Her ass was indeed a tight one. Was Rook's metaphorical ass as tight as Ellen's literal one? It was a philosophical quandary they didn't mind researching.

While the boys ogled her derriere, Rook surveyed the stars above them. It was a cold night, just on the verge of frozen breath. Without city lights to dim them, the moon and the stars illuminated the beach. The moon's pockmarked face was on full display and casting a silver grin over the lake. The air was still and the water gently lapped at the shore in its unending quest to erode the land.

The lake, while well known, was small and secluded, isolated by surrounding forest. Fishermen and boaters able to get their craft in the water from the one dirt road frequented it in the day, but it was undeveloped and thus empty at night, perfect for mis-chievous adolescents who knew the way. Tall pines and hemlocks towered over the small clearing of a beach.

Rook took a swig of the light beer. It was cold and crisp and loosed his muscles as soon as it passed his lips. He wasn't suddenly intoxicated. The brew had an instantaneous psychological effect. Its calming effects were associated with good memories: fishing with Jon, hanging out at the cabin and blasting online enemies with Tatum, and, in a generic sense, independence.

After he had become a legal adult and hit the road, he drifted from town to town, looking for a place to disappear. On his journey he stopped at a few less-than-family-friendly establishments. One of them didn't bother to card him and instead gave him his first beer. He had ordered it on a whim, just to see if he could get away with it, but when he drank the brew, he felt for the first time in his life like a real adult and not just some kid on the road.

Eventually the road brought him to Kyruht and his isolated cabin. Ironically enough, he made more friends and acquaintances in his place of isolation than he had during his entire life before. They drew him out of his protective shell. Mike and Barry had done exactly that this very evening. With some friendly taunting they had coaxed him to a party.

He had never gone to parties in high school. He stayed as invisible as possible, head down and ever forward. There was no need to stop and make friends like Mike and Barry.

He took another swig of his beer. He wasn't an alcoholic, just an avid connoisseur. Both drank regularly, but, unlike the alcoholic, the connoisseur never got drunk.

"Tequila!" Mike shouted to the crowd around the fire and hoisted a precariously large bottle over his head. He looked to Rook with a mischievous grin, "It's time to have some fun."

The twenty-plus voices that had before been a divided chatter merged into a kaleidoscope of laughter and suggestions. The drinking game decided upon was I Have Never. It was much too cold for any games that would get the girls out of their sweaters and jeans, so the guys made the game one of a verbally revealing nature.

Most of the guys appeared to be on Mike's football team. Some even wore their jerseys without any sleeves or coverings, as if immune to the cold. The girls had mostly paired off with the players already. The few that hadn't paired instead grouped together in one impenetrable gaggle of pheromones and estrogen-infused intimidation. The ogled blond named Ellen was in the gaggle.

Mike jumped right in, staring intently at Ellen. "I have never..." He searched, "... gone skinny dipping."

Forced to reveal that they had, in fact, skinny-dipped, over three-fourths of the group drank. Rook imagined that some were just pretending to have dipped in order to seem cool, fit in with the herd, or just for a drink.

After taking the first drink, Mike passed the tequila to the right.

"You realize you're not supposed to make yourself drink, right?" Rook pointed out.

"Yeah, but I wanted one to get rolling with. This bottle will only survive a couple of rounds if eighteen people take a shot every time. Then we'll have to play with beer."

Rook watched as the bottle traveled around the circle they had made. He and Barry were on Mike's left. He wondered what Barry might say when his turn finally came around.

A squirrely boy directly to Mike's right received the bottle after it went full circle. With buckteeth and small hands wrapped greedily around the tequila, he posed a good one. "I have never kissed a member of the same sex."

"This is lame!" someone on the other side of the circle called out.

Several other players grumbled in agreement.

"Goddammit, Tim Tim," Mike said to the squirrel boy half jokingly. "Second statement in and you've lost the group. You know these boys would never incriminate themselves with a drink to that. Too much repressed homosexuality." He spoke just loud enough to call out any cowards nearby. The chicken ploy that had worked so effectively against Rook didn't pull any of the crowd back in. The subject of homosexuality was still too taboo in the small town.

"Fuck it." Mike grabbed the bottle and took a long drink before yelling to the group, "Let's just get fucked up!"

Barry chuckled from under his green beanie as his friend led the charge. He exhaled the last of his contraband and walked to the waterside to flick away the remains.

Someone produced a football and, within seconds, the guys had an intoxicated pick-up game going. It was touch football, but to make it interesting, they had to keep a beer in one hand at all times. The procedure was particularly difficult for receivers, and many good beers were lost, but they managed. Everyone else watched, talked, and drank.

Mike, however, plunged fearlessly into Ellen's gaggle of girls.

Rook leaned to Barry, who had returned to his side. "How can he do that so effortlessly?"

They both watched Mike work. Barry seemed lost in thought, or just too high, because he didn't speak. Still, Rook carried on the conversation.

"People scare the shit out of me. Hell, I was in this town for almost year before I started talking to you guys."

Barry remained silently contemplative.

"Good talk, Barry. Good talk." He dug his hands into his pockets and sighed.

Barry then gave one of the few reminders that he had functioning vocal chords. "I admire him, man."

Startled by Barry's profession, Rook searched the four words for meaning.

"Fucking Ducks," Barry baffled him further.

It wasn't immediately clear, but it eventually dawned on Rook that Barry was referring to ducks with a capital D. Barry was losing his best, lifelong friend to the University of Oregon after graduation. Though they would be relatively close, the drift would be inevitable. Barry could feel it and was already missing his outgoing and sociable friend. The only social skills he had were in dealing, and those interactions were brief and insincere.

Catching Barry's drift, Rook flowed along. "I guess people like you and me live vicariously through people like Mike. The world scares us so we watch from the sideline while they play the game of life, spectators and players. The hard truth, though, is that eventually we all play, whether or not we feel we're ill-equipped."

"The game of life?" Barry laughed.

Rook laughed, too. "Yeah, I guess that was cheesy. You know what I mean, though. And I call myself a writer?"

Barry continued laughing and shook his head. Rook would never hear him speak again.

Firelight flickered against the tree line beside them. The forest was as calm as an abandoned asylum. No bugs clicked, no creatures stirred, and yet it breathed like an organism unto itself. An ethereal energy seemed to hum throughout. Something unseen was lurking beyond and the forest was anxious.

A voice suddenly boomed through a megaphone, "This is the police; time to go home kids. If anyone has been drinking, I will be glad to give you a ride . . ."

Like cockroaches scurrying away from light, they fled the flashing cherries on top of Tatum's cruiser in all directions. Some brave minors ran straight past him to their vehicles along the dirt roads. Most disappeared into the woods to circle around to the road, as if Tatum wouldn't spot them sprinting to their car doors and fumbling with their keys.

Mike, Barry, and Rook didn't move. Mike instead picked up the abandoned tequila bottle and took one last swig.

"C'mon, man. The party barely started!" he addressed Tatum, who was strolling toward them, megaphone in hand.

Standing mere feet away, Tatum pointed the megaphone directly at Mike and spoke again. "I am a *police officer.*" He stretched the words out and pronounced each syllable clearly to emphasize the fact.

Mike dropped the bottle and covered his ears. "Jesus, man!"

Speaking normally, Tatum said, "That's better." He grinned. His eyes then fell to Rook. "And what are you doing here? Aren't you a bit old for this group, Rook?"

"That's what I told him." Rook pointed to Mike.

"It was just some harmless fun, Tate," Mike pleaded his case.

"Officer Tatum," he corrected.

"Deputy," Mike muttered.

"It's harmless fun until I'm scraping one of you kids off the side of the highway and putting you into a dozen separate bags. Then I have to go tell your parents that, because you were just having a little harmless fun, they have to bury you in a closed casket within the week or burn the remains of their only child into ash. So by all means, go ahead."

Mike picked the bottle back up.

"Goddamnit, Mike." Tatum swatted it away again.

"What? You said go ahead."

"You know I wasn't serious."

Rook and Barry quietly watched the exchange. A car that must have fought tooth and nail against the onslaught of teens in the other direction pulled up behind Tatum's cruiser. The driver was a late arrival who apparently didn't mind the presence of law enforcement. Rook recognized the vehicle from outside Shelby's and Distance. It was Dawn.

Mike continued bickering with Tatum. "You won't have to tell Mom and Dad I was killed in a drunk driving accident. You don't have to tell them I was drinking either. Who's your most favorite brother in the world?"

"Half-brother," Tatum reminded him. "Mike, I can't keep letting you slide on this stuff. You're eventually going to have to accept responsibility and learn." He then looked to Barry, who still had a spare joint tucked behind his ear, outside the beanie. "And you, knock that shit off." Tatum grabbed the drug and flicked it into the water.

Barry, who had forgotten about his spare until then, watched, wide-eyed, as his weed took on water and sank. He looked at it like it was a drowning puppy he was helpless to rescue.

Dawn strolled up behind them and gave Tatum a smile. "I miss the party?"

Mike jumped right in. "But we're having a special after party just for you." He winked.

Following a roll of his eyes and a sigh, Tatum instructed Mike, "You're going home." He held out his hand. "Keys."

Mike grumbled and turned them over.

"Barry, how much have you had tonight?"

He shrugged.

"For Pete's sake, guys. All right, fine, get into the back of my car and I'll drive you home."

"But . . ."

"Now Mike." He pointed and scolded. "Listen to your older brother when he has a gun."

"Half-brother," Mike corrected as he and Barry sauntered toward the vehicle.

Tatum turned back to Dawn and Rook.

"Pete's sake? Really?" Rook questioned and then they all laughed a little.

Tatum poked back, "At least I wasn't at a high school party with a bunch of kids I got almost ten years on."

"She came, didn't she?" Rook pointed to Dawn. Then he thought for a moment. "Why did you come?"

She didn't immediately have an answer, but smiled at him coyly. Mike had, of course, invited her, like he always did, but it seemed something else got her to actually attend, fashionably late or not. Rook held back a pleased smile.

"I didn't have anything going on after work tonight, so I just thought I'd check up on the boys and have a drink," she finally answered.

"Well, both of you do me a favor: the next time something is happening that shouldn't be happening, tell me about it."

Dawn moved her hands vertically, then horizontally across her chest and grinned her mischievous grin. "Cross my heart."

With a grin like that, she may as well have been crossing her fingers behind her back.

"Sure thing," Rook agreed, "but what about when we see you doing something you shouldn't be doing?"

"What would that be?" he asked.

"Having a quick drink with Dawn and me while Mike and Barry wait impatiently in the back of the cruiser they don't yet realize they locked themselves into." He pointed to the abandoned cooler containing light beer. "It's our responsibility to confiscate this contraband lest the minors return for it."

"He does have a point," Dawn helped his case.

Tatum caved without a fight. "All right, fine, one drink. Then we dump the cooler and its contents over the fire. I don't want Smokey the Bear up my ass, too. I'm already going to have Sue all over me for letting everyone get away."

In moments the three of them sat shoulder to shoulder on a large log repurposed as a bench near the fire.

Tatum took a drink, "The things I do for my little brother."

"Remind me again how he's your brother?" Dawn asked. "You were several years ahead of me, but I don't remember you having a brother at all when we were in high school."

"Mikey is technically a half-brother, and even though I knew him, we never knew we were related until after I graduated. Long story short, Mike's mom cheated with my dad way back in the day. Luckily, though, Mike's surrogate father loves him like his own regardless. He's a good man, a saint really, for putting up with a kid like Mike."

They laughed, but they all knew Mike was a good kid with a bright future.

Rook proposed a toast and raised his beer in the direction of the cruiser. "To Mike and Barry, they're trouble with a good heart, and without them, we wouldn't be here."

"Fair enough." Tatum stood up and raised his beer. "They still aren't catching any more breaks from me, though."

"Riiiiiiight," Dawn teased. She then pulled out the lighter Rook had given to her and lit a cigarette.

"Cigarettes will kill you, you know." Tatum watched her flick the lighter shut and ignore his advice. "Where'd you get that?"

She wiggled up against Rook and put her head on his shoulder. Her skin was warm and soft as silk. He momentarily closed his eyes and wanted to shut off all his other senses in order to further enjoy and memorize the touch.

"This gentleman here gave it to me."

Tatum looked at Rook and mouthed, "What?"

Rook turned his hands palms up and shook his head, trying desperately not to discourage her from his shoulder while doing so. He wasn't sure what was going on either. Dawn was always playful, but this felt related to the brazen kiss.

"I, uh . . ." To his dismay she sat back up in her own space. "I got it from Jon. He pretty much forced me to take it." It wasn't a straight lie and it sounded like a joke, perfectly non-incriminating. He hadn't really stolen it and intended to pay, but it was still for the best that they didn't know its origins. He would give Jon a generous sum when he honored his drink request the following evening. After Rook returned the message he'd left, Jon invited him to discuss the wolf carving over drinks.

The wolf carving and the creature from his dreams had escaped his mind while with his friends. He'd forgotten completely until Jon popped up. A nagging feeling told Rook that his nocturnal problems and Jon's reaction were based on something more than super-stition and coincidence.

A rear door to the cop car bounced in its frame and they could hear yelling.

"Looks like they figured out we left them locked in." Tatum laughed. "I'd better take them home. You two can go ahead and take what you want, but douse the fire with the water in the cooler." On the fate of the beer, too, he had conceded.

"I'll save a few for our next game night." Rook pulled several out and balanced them on the log.

Dawn didn't take any. She instead spoke as she dumped her half-consumed beer in the fire. "You boys and your games."

"You girls and your games." Rook emphasized "your" and looked at Dawn.

"Oh, whatever. Dangling a few suitors around to find the best is different than blasting someone's head off in an online death match," she defended.

Tatum chimed in. "Yeah, but ours is more humane."

Rook wondered if he was on one of Dawn's hooks and poured the cooler's icy slush over the bonfire. Thick, gray smoke billowed up from the drowned embers.

Chapter 11

Carnival music echoed through the vacant amusement park. There were no children running and laughing. There were no screams of joy on the empty rollercoaster or Ferris wheel. The "doo doodoodoodoo-doodoo doo doodoo" cracking out of the speaker boxes was the only sound being made.

Rook wasn't sure how he'd gotten there or why, but something seemed familiar about the amusement park. He tried to remember where he'd seen the game stalls, winding rollercoaster, swirling log flumes, cotton candy vendors, and all the other novelties before.

He walked down the barren paths littered with paper cups, plates, straws, foil, and cigarette butts. He smelled hot dogs, funnel cake, and pizzas in the air. Yet he saw no one. It was as if the amusement park was operating itself. He heard the sound of helium hissing out of a tank and into thin rubber balloons.

Following the source of the hissing led him directly beneath the Ferris wheel. He realized how he knew the park. The Ferris wheel was the very one he'd ridden with Darla Cartwright when he was ten and his then-foster parents were trying to socialize him. He tried conquering his fear of heights to impress her, but ended up spewing his fear over the side of the basket when the two of them had made it to the top. She wasn't impressed.

What struck him even more than the Ferris wheel was the clown filling up balloons at the base. The clown had a bright red afro wig, a dirty blue shirt, white-and-orange-spotted oversized overalls with black stains, huge red shoes, and the standard red nose. His white grease face paint was smeared on haphazardly, his lips and eyes were black, his toothy grin was yellow, and black tentacles wriggled out from various holes in his attire. The saliva between his teeth looked like old engine oil.

Rook thought to himself, *I've fallen asleep. I'm dreaming.* He couldn't remember how he'd gotten home or when he went to sleep.

As if reading his thoughts, the clown said, "Oh, I'm more real than you know, Rookie."

The clown was the same creature that had invaded Rook's dream the prior evenings. The creature was more complete, yet remained unfamiliar. The face paint obscured any chance of seeing a known, human face. A feeling pitted in Rook's stomach told him that he'd become all too acquainted with the creature before long.

The clown stared at him with a malicious grin. The darkened sky over the amusement park took on a reddish tint, cumulus clouds billowed heavily above, and a gust of wind picked up the trash littered on the pavement.

A thought occurred to Rook. "Are you . . ." He paused. "Grey?"

The clown laughed and threw his head back. "Is that what you think? I'm another one of your fictional characters?" He laughed harder. "Go ahead, call me Grey."

"What else would you be but a figment of my imagination? I mean, you look like 'IT,' after all."

"You've read too many horror stories and watched too many movies, boy." He paused. "Movies . . ." He raised a white, gloved hand to his chin. Brown fingernails poked out of holes in the pointer and ring finger. "Wondrous invention; they're playgrounds for violence, rage, anger, pain, suffering . . . fear. It's amazing how much you people let yourself get into them, how much you become a part of the fantasy and feed the darkness."

Rook didn't respond and, after a brief standoff of silence, the clown spoke again. "What's the matter,

Rookie? Don't you like this place?" The clown cackled and threw his head back once more. He stopped abruptly and stared at Rook, head tilted to the side, grin wide. He stepped forward. He picked up a large, heavy carnival mallet that had been leaning against the balloon stand and let it hang near his side. The mallet was scratched and abraded and speckled with blood.

"Your dreams really are something, Rookie. They're the perfect place for me to incubate."

The clown's use of the word "incubate" made him feel as if his brain had become home to some alien parasite comfortably nestled above his cerebellum, poking around with dagger-like protrusions.

It laughed again. "I'm no parasite. I'm not saying your brain is healthy. Do you think normal people dream like you do? You're a freak." He paused. "But the perfect freak for me." The clown grinned, slung the mallet behind his shoulders, and rested his arms on top in a crucifix position. The clown slowly walked toward him.

"What do you want?" Rook stepped backward, careful to keep his eye on the clown.

"Ah! You want answers?! But I can't. That would ruin all the fun of the surprise!" Without so much as another step forward, the clown was suddenly in front of Rook, nose to red nose." Abub bub bub, how did you do that, Mr. Clown?" He mocked what Rook was thinking and let out his self-pleased cackle.

The clown tilted his head again to study him. Rook could see every yellow, rotted tooth in the twisted smile. He could smell decaying and burning flesh on the clown's breath. The scent stung his eyes and choked his airways. The face under the paint looked like someone he knew, someone close to him.

"You gotta start thinking outside the box, Rookie." It grabbed him and crushed him with what looked like a hug but felt like a vice-grip clamped tight to the point of bones snapping. The clown whispered in his ear, "I can do whatever I want." He stepped back and stretched his arms wide. "Hell, I made this whole carnival out of your thoughts and memories."

It disappeared again and Rook dropped to his knees in pain. The fetid flesh and burnt sulfur smell clung to his clothing. He felt at his sides, sure to find ribs poking out. He couldn't breathe deeply and every shallow breath felt like a knife shredding his insides. He scanned the carnival for signs of the clown.

"Over here!" the clown yelled giddily. It jumped up and down, slapping its knees from on top of the station where The Beast rolled to rest. In a suddenly solemn, raspy voice, it declared, "I'll give you one surprise." It tapped the mallet against the roof of the station and roared in laughter again.

The roller coaster, which had been chugging along by itself, rounded the final turn and braked to a stop in the station. In the front seat Carol and Richard sat limp and lifeless. They were from a time too painful to remember. Their bodies were undamaged, but their skulls had been caved in like pumpkins. There were no faces, only a bloody mess of splintered bone and a lower jaw. On Richard's corpse an unpopped eyeball dangled by a jagged tooth.

Seeing the only parents he had ever loved in all his unstable years pulverized to a pulp was nauseating, but he didn't want to give the clown the satisfaction he seemed to be looking for. It was just a dream, he told himself, and they were long dead anyway.

"You cold-hearted orphan!" the clown sobbed into his shoulder. "Wait, I have an idea!" He placed his thumb in his mouth and blew as if inflating a balloon. As he did, the bloody mess that was the heads of Carol and Richard began to inflate. Bone, teeth, and the remaining eyeball fell away, leaving basketball-sized, flesh-colored sacks pulsing with life that Rook didn't want to see.

With a turn of his wrist and wiggle of his fingers, the two corpses pulled themselves out of the front car and trotted down the platform, surprisingly surefooted for creatures without eyes or ears. When they had made it onto the main path, no more than six feet from Rook, the clown clenched his open palm into a fist. They stopped obediently. The clown made a gun with his hand and fired with two flicks of his thumb.

The pulsating sacks ripped open and thousands of leeches slithered out. The frenzied bloodsuckers were as large as snakes and as black as his nightmares. The slime-coated vampires slid down their necks toward the ground, but didn't venture off. They instead completely covered the legs, torso, and arms of the bodies. They were eating the corpses. More startling yet was the fact that, within the emptied sacks, new faces had sprouted and were crying out in agony. Whatever power the clown possessed immobilized Carol and Richard, and they were left to be devoured by the hungry swarm of leeches. They looked in wide-eyed terror at Rook as they screamed.

His stomach turned and vomit rose in his throat. He choked it back. Frustration swelled in his chest.

As if being embraced by a warm wintertime fire, the clown rolled its eyes back and sighed in enjoyment. "Not only fear but anger! I love it!"

This was Rook's second reality, a place as true to him as the waking world. Two people he had loved dearly and attempted to preserve in memory were being eaten alive in front of him, and there was nothing he could do to stop it. He repeated himself, "What do you want?"

"I want to go for a ride . . ."

As if the clown had opened his brain and planted the idea, Rook knew exactly what ride he wanted to take.

"No . . ." Rook's voice was light, like that of a child.

Just as the clown had flashed around the amusement park at will, so, too, did the snowy highway flash into being.

Rook could feel the cold air against his skin and see the glistening asphalt of the highway strewn with wreckage leading over a guardrail.

"This was a rough night, wasn't it, Rookie?" a voice cackled.

The clown was nowhere to be seen and yet was everywhere. Rook could feel the evil energy clouding the dream, surrounding him as it previously had.

"You won't show me the fat man, but this memory

is almost as powerful. You remember everything, don't you? Every detail of the night you killed your blood parents?"

Rook clenched his hands and then realized they were those of a child. He was a boy again. He stammered, "It wasn't my fault. I didn't do it."

Warm tears built in his eyes and wet the tops of his cheeks. He even had the emotional fortitude of a child again.

"Aw, poor baby. Too bad you killed your mommy. Otherwise, she could hold her little baby!" the voice taunted him.

"They deserved it . . ." Rook said through a muffled sob, then added, ". . . *he* did."

"Why are you crying, little boy?! You shouldn't feel guilt if they deserved it." The voice paused. Rook swore he could hear it breathing. "That's not all, though, is it? You're *still* angry. You'd kill them all over again, wouldn't you? Accept it! You're a killer!"

"I didn't kill them! It was their fault!" Rook's child voice yelled across the quiet highway.

"What about the fat man, hmm? I know you'd love to jam something sharp into one ear and out the other, or maybe slit his throat below those disgusting chins. How about it, Rookie?"

He fell to his knees and buried his face in his hands. "Never . . . I will never go near the fat man again. Not even to kill him!"

"WHY?! What is the fat man to you?! What did he do?!" The voice boomed along the highway and hit Rook like a wall. "I've read his description, but I need the story!"

"GET OUT OF MY HEAD!" Rook screamed out. He wanted no more. The ground began to shake and the asphalt cracked like eggshell. Chunks heaved upward while others fell away entirely. Boulders tumbled down the mountainside and moonlight disappeared from the sky. Lightning exploded out of the dark abyss overhead and thunder roared in approval.

From behind he heard the voice whisper through the chaos into his ear, "Fight all you want. Your special little mind will be mine. You will weaken. Death eats at resolve . . . I will break you . . ."

As soon as the voice had finished, lightning ripped the sky in two. The dream itself fractured like glass and Rook woke up screaming.

He shot upright in bed as if the explosive force of the dream had flung him from one world into the next. His chest heaved and his breaths escaped him like he'd just run a marathon. The sweat-soaked sheets were clenched tightly in his hands.

After several minutes of collecting his mind in the dark, he let his arms give out beneath him and his back fell to the now-cold, wet sheets. He lay there with his eyes open and listened as Tank approached. The bed swayed as Tank jumped onto it. He wasn't allowed, but Rook hadn't the strength to push him away, nor did he really want to. Tank lay next to him and, after a nuzzle, rested his soft, furry head on Rook's stomach.

Rook could hear the massive dog whimpering in the darkness.

Chapter 12

Dr. Harper's one-man clinic was quaint and efficient. He had a single exam room for patients, the lobby where his secretary/nurse camped behind a desk, and his office for paperwork and the occasional consultation. Rook awaited his consultation in an old wooden chair with a blue, patchwork cushion; there was no special black leather sofa on which to recline. A second wooden chair remained empty to his left. The walls were decorated with a few color-saturated paintings of Mediterranean villas and a world of wine, cheese, and caviar. Harper probably vacationed in such places when he wasn't trapped in middle-of-nowhere Oregon. Rook favored the middle of nowhere.

The door to the office opened. "Sorry to keep you waiting. Mrs. Cornwell did have her appointment first."

"No problem. I appreciate you seeing me on such short notice."

"So what's wrong? You look healthy enough to me." The doctor cut to the chase. His busy schedule was apparent.

"Well, physically I'm fit as a fiddle."

Dr. Harper got situated behind his desk. Pictures of his children populated the surface. "I don't like how you emphasized physically." He tapped the side of his head.

Rook responded, "I'm not schizo, I don't think anyway."

"Then what's the problem?"

"My dreams . . ." Rook trailed off.

Dr. Harper leaned back in his chair, which creaked slightly under the strain. Harper wasn't obese. On the contrary, he was a healthy, full-sized man. He was five ten with thick arms and a flat stomach toned by a healthy lifestyle and more trips to the gym than a priest makes to the altar. He practiced what he preached. He had large hands that lent more to a boxer than they would to the delicate work he required of them. No one in town had complained of sloppy stitches. Rook wondered how he managed to provide prostate exams with fingers like bananas.

"What about your dreams?"

"Ever since the, uh, incident, my dreams have been different than most people's." He gauged Dr. Harper's reaction and then unloaded. "I'm completely aware in my dreams and control them. It's like a whole other reality."

Harper raised an eyebrow, no doubt questioning Rook's self-proclaimed sanity. "Some dreams can seem very real. It's not uncommon."

"I'm not just talking about a few realistic dreams, though. Every dream I have I'm actually *there* inside my head, talking to my characters, living and breathing."

The doctor didn't seem sure how to react. "I'm not a neurologist, Rook. You might want to have your head checked out."

"That's not the problem."

"It isn't?" Harper was wondering what trumped delirium. The inquisitive nature of the doctor in him took over. "So what is the problem?"

"Lately there's been someone else in my dreams, someone not like my characters, someone with a consciousness like you and me. And it's made my dreams into nightmares."

"You're telling me that some intelligent being like you and me has infiltrated your dreams, which are more than dreams."

"When you say it, I sound crazy."

"You do sound crazy."

He sighed. "I'm serious, though, Dr. Harper. I keep seeing this thing whenever I close my eyes. I feel like it's inside of me, right on the verge of my conscious mind."

"Rook, I think you should go up to Berryville and

get examined by the neurologists at the hospital. When was your last scan?" Harper thumbed through his file.

"About six months after what happened."

"Six months after the accident was your last scan?" The doctor was shocked. "That was over fifteen years ago!"

It wasn't really an "accident," thought Rook.

Dr. Harper studied him carefully and then sighed. "In the few years you have been here I have never known you to be irrational, but this story . . . I can call up and arrange for you to get a new scan if you'd like. Given the trauma you suffered, you could have some sort of damage, physical or mental, even so many years later. Your scans never showed anything wrong, but it doesn't mean your doctors didn't miss something."

"I guess I don't have much choice."

Harper thought for a moment. "It was the back of your head, wasn't it?"

Rook only hesitated for a second before he knew what the doctor was talking about. "Felt like my head exploded everywhere, but yeah, that's where the brunt of the damage was, according to the doctors who put me back together."

"Have you ever heard of Charcot-Wilbrand syndrome?"

Rook looked at him like he was speaking Egyptian. "Damn it, man. I'm a writer, not a doctor!" He knew Harper had a penchant for Star Trek and, as planned, the twist on the catchphrase got a chuckle from Harper.

The doctor squelched any further laughter and sobered up. "Charcot-Wilbrand syndrome involves the supposed dream center of the brain. Scientists don't know exactly how it works but after trauma to a specific region in the back of the brain, normally due to stroke, some patients have lost the ability to dream altogether. It's only been documented in a handful of patients. Now theoretically damage to the 'dream center' . . ." –he put imaginary quotes on the two words to emphasize just how hypothetical the dream center was—". . . could work the other way and heighten the dream in the way

75

you feel you've experienced." He waited for Rook to absorb the information.

Rook stared at him, through him, in thought.

"Or the simpler explanation is that you have suffered some sort of mental break, most likely brought on by what happened finally catching up to you. I believe it is more likely a mental issue rather than physical damage, which is why I'm going to give you the name of a good psychiatrist to consult after you get another scan." He pulled out a pad of notepaper and scribbled a name and phone number on it. "I want you to take this seriously and really go see her. You're a good heart and the town is happy to have you. We can't have you losing your marbles now."

"Just call me Toodles," Rook joked.

After a small smile, Harper pressed him, "Promise me you'll go see Victoria for a full psychological evaluation if nothing shows on your scan. You got me concerned with this dream business." He handed Rook one of his cards with the phone number and address for Victoria's practice scribbled on the back.

"Uh, Doc, this is in Portland," Rook pointed out.

"It's a trek, but she's worth it, if just for an eval."

The missing hikers came to Rook's mind. "Yeah, it's quite a hike to Portland."

Dr. Harper didn't miss the hint. "I'm not supposed to share that information with anyone outside the investigation."

"Ah, c'mon. It was right by my place. I live alone out in the woods. I'd like to know what's lurking out there. Besides, who am I going to tell?" He repeated, "I live alone in the woods."

The doctor sighed and gave in much easier than Rook expected. He wanted to talk. "All right, I'll tell you what I observed just so you know how careful you need to be until they catch the guy." He paused and gave a disclaimer. "You didn't hear this from me."

Rook pinched his lips together tight to signify he wouldn't talk.

Harper leaned back in his chair and tapped his

fingers against his desk. "Someone has an extreme problem. From what I can tell, Mitchell, the hiker we found, was attacked with a large knife and stabbed at least a dozen times before the murderer tore apart the remains. Whoever did it wasn't satisfied with merely killing and took to dismantling. There was a great deal of anger and frustration unleashed on poor Mitch."

"That's awful. You think it was the other hiker?"

"Honestly? No. They were friends. This was an attack of pure rage. I don't think anyone, no matter what occurred, could tear the body of their friend apart with their bare hands. It doesn't seem humanly possible to me. Although, I guess people are capable of some pretty terrible things."

Chapter 13

Rook was in no rush to visit Berryville per Dr. Harper's request. His nightmares were vivid, and "Grey" was a hell of a boogeyman, but he had endured worse. After the accident, he spent more time than he cared to relive in the hospital. The last several days' worth of spooks and oddities were just the product of his overactive imagination. If they weren't, well, he could endure longer before he paid the old germ factory a visit. A visit to Jon's seemed more important. It felt like the place he needed to be.

The obsidian wolf sat on the table in front of him, forever stoic in its frozen pose. As magnificent as the figurine was, Rook couldn't help but feel like something dark was seeping out of it. The empty black eyes of the wolf stared back and examined *him* with equal curiosity. It looked as if it were carefully examining prey, looking for weaknesses. Rook turned the figurine sideways, facing the wall against which Jon's table rested.

Jon returned to the table and Rook eagerly shifted his attention away from the figurine. Jon had brought a pitcher of iced tea and two scotch glasses.

"We're drinking tea out of these?" Rook picked up the scotch glass.

"Who said this is tea?" Jon grinned and wrinkles filled his forehead. "This is a hard herbal drink my grandmother taught me how to brew when I was but a colt." He poured Rook's glass first. It was hard to tell if he was serious or pandering when he referred to himself as a "colt."

"Great woman. What's in it?"

"You don't want to know." Jon poured his glass second. "Cheers."

"To grandma." Rook raised his glass.

After a clank, they both took long swigs. Rook immediately regretted the decision and decided he'd sip the rest of the drink. It tasted like whiskey, mint, and a variety of herbs he would never be able to identify, but did have the enjoyable side effect of putting warmth in his veins. His tongue felt singed after.

"Jesus, Jon. Why'd you bring us a whole pitcher of that stuff?"

"It's for good luck."

"That's a lot of good luck."

Jon stared solemnly at Rook for a moment. In that instant, he looked like the ancient Shasta that Rook had seen in pictures. He was a strong man whose tan skin and long, black hair stayed true to his proud roots. Crows feet had started to creep into the corners of his eyes, but they still glistened with decades of life to come. When those eyes shifted to the figurine, something else lurked behind them, something that disconcerted Rook.

"I want to apologize for the other day. You caught me off-guard when you brought the wolf into my shop. I have better protection here."

Protection? Rook's mind buzzed with Jon's reference. Jon felt the power behind the wolf, the darkness, just as Rook did.

Rook decided to prod for confirmation, "The wolf. . . . Why does it scare you?"

"You feel it, don't you? You know it is to be feared. You look at it with the same eyes." Jon paused. "Rook, there is a story you should hear, the story of my ancestors."

Rook listened with hungry ears. He always enjoyed a good story from Jon. However, Jon didn't seem as excited. He took another big drink.

"Before I begin, you should understand that my people believe that all the emotions and all the feelings we experience, which make us who we are, come from two roots: love and fear. Everything we do boils down to love or fear. Everything we are is love or fear." He looked at the wolf apprehensively and took another drink.

Rook drank again as a sign of good faith. When he followed Jon's eyes, he realized that the wolf was facing him again. "Did you just . . ."

Jon interrupted him, "Many centuries ago the great warrior Chief Klamath had three sons: Idakariuke, Ikaruck, and Kosetah. They grew stronger and healthier every passing year until they were the fiercest warriors this land has ever known. They fought many battles for their father but did not share his desire for conquest. They sought a peaceful, sedentary life and not the nomadic warrior way. Chief Klamath blamed their mother, the kind and noble Umpqua. He accused her of softening the hearts of his warriors and had her tied to a boulder, which was dropped into the depths of the great mountain lake. The brothers were enraged and, after the near-assassination of their own father, swore instead to never fight or wage war again. They left his tribe, and terrified not only by their father's rage but their own, sought to rid themselves of all that was fear. Sorrow, misery, anger, rage, fury—they attempted to remove all evils from within and swore to live by the love of their mother."

Jon stopped once more and stared at the wolf. His hand fidgeted at the edge of the table.

"The Shasta are descended from the three brothers. They made us a people of peace, under the blessing of the Great Creator and the land he had given, and we prospered in this same wilderness for lifetimes before the white man came. Since then, my people have nearly disappeared. Only a handful of us remain, but we persist peacefully and live off the land as much as we can."

"So what does the figurine have to do with that?"

"For each of the three brothers there is an artifact said to contain the Fear they removed from their being. I believe that wolf to be one of those artifacts."

Rook thought for a second and picked up the wolf. "You mean this small, obsidian carving contains ancient fear, or, in other words, all that is wrong and evil?"

"Yes . . ."

"Suppose it really does harbor some dark force your forefathers sealed away. What's to keep it from getting out?" Rook twirled the wolf in his fingers. The darkness he had felt oozing out had disappeared. His previous apprehension seemed unfounded now that he heard the ridiculous story. It was more than ridiculous; it was frustrating being spoon-fed bullshit like some fool. Rook could feel an unreal anger creeping through his veins, but it wasn't his. He wasn't mad at Jon. He enjoyed the stories. He didn't know where the sudden anger was coming from. It seemed unfounded. He sniffled and tasted blood.

"I'm glad you asked. The artifacts were hidden away and my people guarded them. Over time, and through generations, their location was forgotten. Those of us who still knew the story doubted it. I myself didn't believe it until I saw, and felt, the wolf. I must ask you to relinquish it to me so I may hide it once more in our sacred lands and sacred waters. It cannot be destroyed, only released, which is why I must contain it."

Rook smiled. "So you know where to take it so the evil never escapes?"

Jon nodded.

"Perfect." The voice was no longer Rook's but a deep, raspy hiss. The smile became a malicious grin.

Before Jon could act, Rook's arm shot across the small table and clamped tightly on Jon's forearm. The herbal drink sloshed and both glasses rolled off the table.

"Who are you?" Jon remained poised.

"I have no one name, but you know me. I am fear. I am anger. I am fury. I am rage." The pseudo-Rook paused thoughtfully. "There is a persona Rook has tried to define me with." His voice echoed with a ferocious conviction that bordered on a snarl. "I am Grey, and I am more!" He seemed angered by attempted definition. "I am evil in its purest form."

Understanding shook Jon to his core. He whispered the name his grandfather had told him in stories once dismissed as fantasy, the very meaning of which was darkness, "Apxutaraxi."

Apxutaraxi's hand crushed Jon's forearm with all the strength Rook's muscles offered. Jon tried to keep from showing the pain. He would give Apxutaraxi no satisfaction.

Jon looked into Apxutaraxi's eyes. "Rook, you must take the artifact to the deep . . ."

His words trailed off in the blood seeping below his neck. Apxutaraxi had pulled a jade pocketknife with Rook's other hand and sliced Jon's throat in one swift maneuver.

"Ooooh. You didn't like that, did you, Rook? I can hear you in there. I can feel your anger. Embrace it!" Apxutaraxi shouted. "Feed it! Let it grow! Give me strength!" He cackled ecstatically.

Jon slumped to the floor and watched with fading life as Apxutaraxi picked up the pitcher and slurped a large drink. The brown liquid sloshed out of the cracks of his mouth and poured down Rook's white shirt. "By the way, Jon, you got the recipe wrong."

Chapter 14

Rook awoke, slumped against the inner frame of the front door. Beside him were a smeared line of red clay dust and a line of salt bordering it on one side. He hadn't noticed it on the way in to see Jon. Rook remembered Jon and climbed to his feet, nearly knocked down again when Apxutaraxi's voice slammed through his head.

That damn Redskin couldn't even get the barrier right. We're trapped INSIDE.HAHAHAHAHA!

"Apxutaraxi?!Get out!" Rook grabbed his throbbing head in his hands.

Love to, but that half-baked Indian trapped us in with dirt that was meant to keep me out!

His first instinct was to go to Jon, see if he was alive, and call for help, but he knew Jon was dead and lifeless on the floor. He could see Jon in his mind, the way Apxutaraxi had seen him. The scene was blurry like a frantic dream, but he remembered watching hands, his hands, hold Jon, and cut his throat. The blood on his hands and jeans verified the nightmare.

Rook could feel Apxutaraxi pacing the back of his mind like a tiger trapped in a cage. He leaned back against the frame to regain control of his fractured mind and dropped his hands to his side. His left hand crossed over the powder line and into blazing hot embers. He felt the skin immediately burn and peel away, exposing the tender flesh beneath to the hot blast.

Apxutaraxi screamed in unison with him as he pulled his hand back to find that it had not been incinerated. On his side of the line the pain vanished.

Aaaaaagh! You ignorant bastard!

Apxutaraxi roared inside him. He could hear heavy, exhaled breath followed by hissing inhalation. He realized the breathing noises were coming from him.

"Fuck you, Apxutaraxi!" He stepped across the line. The bones in his leg exploded. Fire was melting his flesh from the inside out. Molten lead seemed to surge up to his hip. He cried out to God, one he hadn't thought he believed in, as the pain ravaged him. Sobs mixed with the screams. Tears ran down his face. He hadn't cried since the night his parents died. He'd thought nothing would ever bring him to tears again, but the pain, the pain was a hundred times more excruciating than anything he'd ever felt before.

He collapsed back into the sanctuary of Jon's home.

Apxutaraxi's screams turned into gasping laughter and then, eventually, faded into silence.

Rook knew what still lurked inside him. He would have to find another way to deal with Apxutaraxi, though. The door wasn't going to work. It may have killed Apxutaraxi if he stayed in the fire long enough, but it was impossible to bear.

He stumbled back to Jon's body in the dining room. The orange shag carpet was stained dark red, the fibers thick with blood. Jon's corpse lay unmoved where he had fallen. His long, dark hair was spread out. His white feather still held. Rook went to him and placed two fingers just below his jaw where a warm pulse ought to be. Instead, he found a cold, unmoving artery. A deep gash penetrated across Jon's neck just below his fingers. The jugular had been severed and Jon bled out almost instantly.

With his fingers still dug in below Jon's jaw, Rook noticed the black veins on the back of his hand. They were unmistakable. *Fucking Benedict*, thought Rook, or was it Apxutaraxi who had been messing with him that day, telling him what was inevitable?

He couldn't wait there with the body until someone came looking. He didn't kill Jon, but no one would believe in Apxutaraxi. He could hear the townspeople: "That weird Rook guy finally snapped. I knew he was messed up in the head!"

Jon couldn't have sealed every entrance and exit. He would've only been testing Rook coming through the front door. He couldn't have been suspecting an attack, although he should have.

Rook first checked the windows on the ground floor, then the back door, and the basement. They all had a red and white line in front of them. Jon had indeed been anticipating the worst. If Rook knew what Apxutaraxi was capable of, he wouldn't have come to test Jon's defenses. Guilt outweighed his desperation. He stopped to look at Jon's lifeless body once more. It was all too surreal. He killed a man. Perhaps not directly, but it wasn't the first time he was responsible for the death of a human being, except, this time, Jon didn't deserve it. He was a kindly old Native who did little more than etch out a modest living, contribute to Barry's customer base, and share laughs with friends. Jon made everyone around him smile. There would be no more smiling from Jon.

The anger that was becoming a trend crept up inside Rook's stomach with fingers like daggers. The anger traveled upward still to his lungs and chest. Swelling with the wave of emotion, he did not sob for Jon. He clenched his right hand tightly and slammed it hard against the wall with a mixture of grunts and screams. The old drywall caved beneath his fist, leaving a small, circular hole between the studs.

An idea occurred to him. Jon kept an ax just inside the back door. He used it to chop wood but wouldn't leave it outside to the elements. Like many of his buys, he bragged about it. He was as proud of his ax as his grandfather was of his tomahawk and rifle. It was a double bit forged from high carbon tool steel with a fiberglass resin-coated oak handle and a rubber grip. Some desperate patron sold it to him for next to nothing. A good ax was a commodity in Kyruht. Hung on the arm of a coat rack with no coats, the ax was easy to spot next to the back door.

He returned to the dining area and planted his feet shoulder width apart on the orange shag. He tapped the flat side of the head against the dirty yellow drywall to determine how much space was between the studs.

The first swing sank in deep, effortlessly. The second struck one of the studs. He wasn't exactly Paul Bunyan and he would have to eventually break through the stud anyway so the inaccuracy didn't deter him.

Fucking powder.

The thought wasn't entirely his. The anger toward Jon's precautions, like the anger that crept in during Jon's story, wasn't his. He could feel Apxutaraxi writhing around inside him like a snake desperately trying to escape a burlap sack. Apxutaraxi's tentacles stretched through his extremities, not currently in control, but laying in wait like idle fingers tapping in anticipation.

Sweat beaded on his forehead and bits of drywall exploded with every swing. He began to imagine the layered yellow paint as skin and the drywall as tissue sliced like butter with the ax. The studs were bone that splintered with each hit. Red, syrupy blood oozed from the half man-sized hole he'd created. The chunks on the floor had become flesh, bits of which were on his shoes.

He swung as hard as he could through the gaping wound and the ax broke through the siding. The hole returned to drywall and wooden studs. The blood disappeared. Still, Jon's body remained.

There were fingerprints all over the place, his saliva was most likely washed back into some of the iced tea, and someone in town most certainly knew he had a visit with Jon. It was small town code that everyone knew what everyone else was up to. Renelette probably saw the disturbance at the pawnshop the other day, and certainly saw Rook hurry out, but he was a conspiracy theorist. Would authorities give credence to his finger pointing when Jon didn't show up to work for several days? What about when they found Jon's corpse, partially decayed by the time they come to look, and ascertained that he had been entertaining company, albeit from the other side of strange lines of dust, when he met his untimely demise?

Rook had some damage control to do if he was going to stay a free man long enough to figure things out. Although he hadn't noticed it before the murder, most likely Apxutaraxi's work, he could feel the pocketknife in his pantsuit was undoubtedly bathed in blood. After a few more swings to widen the hole he had made, he tossed the ax outside. Retracing his steps, he grabbed every bit of incriminating evidence he could think of. The tea glasses had both spilled, but the pitcher was still about a third the way full of "good luck." He dumped it into the shag carpet. Kyruht law enforcement could pull prints, but he doubted they had the CSI capabilities to extract minute amounts of saliva from tea that had been absorbed into the many fibers of the carpet. Even if they called someone in from the Berryville department, retrieval would still be a long shot, and that was if saliva was even discernible within the tea.

Jon deserved a proper burial, but Rook couldn't alert anyone. He draped a sheet over the body and consoled himself in the knowledge that, when Jon was eventually found, they would take him to his family plot. Until then, however, his body would have to bear the elements newly released by the gaping hole in the wall and hopefully avoid meeting scavengers hungry enough to climb into the house.

He found a rag and wiped any would-be prints off the table and doors he had touched. He then wrapped the knife in the rag, put the glasses inside the pitcher, pocketed the wolf, and carefully squeezed through the hole he'd created. It was with an eerie calm he completed all of this. He did have the resolve to avoid punishment for a crime that wasn't truly his, but he knew it was Apxutaraxi who steeled his nerves and guided his steps. Whatever Apxutaraxi was, he seemed to have a sense of self-preservation. At least, he attributed it to Apxutaraxi.

It was dark outside. The sun had been waning when he had arrived. Cold, dark night had fallen with the swiftness of a predator choking out the last rays of light. The air was deathly still. The woods were silent. No animals chuffed or insects buzzed. The trees knew a killer walked among them. Or it seemed so to Rook. The silence was mocking him, taunting him. People may not have known what he did, but nature did, spirits did. The only noise that issued dutifully was the soft crunch of decayed leaves and twigs under his feet has he walked to his truck, guilt in his hands and pockets.

Chapter 15

Barry didn't attend any of the social events at school. Dances, plays, and football games weren't his thing, so when homecoming rolled around on Saturday night, he kept a safe distance. With headphones on and iPod blaring tunes from his favorite bands, he left his home, tragically only blocks away from the school, and strolled by on his way to the junkyard.

Mike and his fellow football players would undoubtedly be going over plans to spike the punch or get the hot Spanish teacher to dance, but the girls of the school would be all made up in their best dresses and polished with makeup. The potential for eye candy was worth the walk by.

Sure enough, Mike was leaned against a pick-up truck, surrounded by teammates. When he saw Barry walking by, Mike smiled and waved him over. Barry smiled back but shook his head and gave the peace sign while still in stride. They both knew full well that Barry was not the type of guy to hang out in front of the school at a dance. The girls, meanwhile, loved it. There were only a hundred girls in grades nine through twelve, most from surrounding towns, and every one of them was present.

Barry continued to walk while inconspicuously checking out the girls. A pretty redhead in a light turquoise dress caught his eye first. He quickly recognized her as Morgan Isabella, a junior, and the contrast between her hair and the dress worked well. He spotted a few other girls he was fond of in the group. Birds of a feather flocked together.

In another gaggle across the front stairs from Morgan

were the twins, Lacy and Lucy. They were sultry blonds who didn't have a piece of clothing in their wardrobe that wasn't skintight. They were also among the most sought-after by the normal boys at the school. Barry figured that odds were they'd end up at the hotel just outside of town by night's end. He didn't understand why all the guys would go after the twins with their bleach blond hair, gaudy sunglasses, cell phones that were perpetually fused to one hand, and propensity for STDs when there were diamonds in the rough like Morgan.

He sighed and kicked at a twig on the sidewalk. After a couple of kicks, he snapped it by stepping directly on it. He watched as a gust caught some leaves and twirled them through the air. A chill ran up his spine. He flipped songs on his iPod and tucked it back into the front pocket of his hoodie. His hands stayed in the pocket for warmth.

The football field was vacant and almost completely dark, save the soft glow of the crescent moon overhead. It was eerie seeing a place that was usually robust with energy, noise, and exuberance completely devoid of life. The white yard lines and boundary markers glowed with a ghostly luminescence.

Barry walked across the field diagonally, loitering near mid-field. The homecoming game had been the previous night. Checking over his shoulder, he turned toward the woods on the away team side of the field. With his back to the school he unzipped and urinated on the fifty-yard line.

Relieved and feeling successfully rebellious, he zipped up and proceeded toward the junkyard. He made a mental note to warn Mike against getting tackled on the south side of mid-field if at all possible.

The junkyard was fenced off twenty yards after the far end zone. In the corner of the fence line near the woods was a clean-cut hole, covered with a leaning sheet of metal and three rubber tires. Opportunistic trailblazers before him had snipped the chain link and used the ancient pile of junk to cover the hole. Every year knowledgeable seniors would share the location with a few underclassmen and the traditional smokers lounge lived on. In the corner of the junkyard, hidden behind a few stacks of debris, was their sanctuary. The old Beck brothers didn't have a "Chopper" in their junk heap to sniff out intruders and scare them away and most likely wouldn't have cared enough even if they did know about the lounge.

Barry sat down cross-legged on the hood of a rusty, trashed '66 Lincoln Continental. The Lincoln served as seating, as did tires and random hunks of metal. The inside of the Lincoln was still accessible and usually remained dry except in the hardest rainstorms. It had been home to many joint operations, both smoking and sexual escapades. He thought fondly about the time he had introduced Rochelle to the Lincoln.

He unrolled a Ziploc bag of weed and pulled a small, silver box out of the side pocket of his cargo pants. Cushioned in the box he had a bubbler that was prepped to go and corked to prevent spillage. He loaded the bowl, as he'd done a thousand times before, and grabbed his trusty Zippo. The first drag was rough due to residual ash in the tube, but the hits got progressively smoother.

As his buzz increased, he relaxed back against the cracked windshield of the Lincoln. When leaves and twigs crunched in the distance, he looked to the forest. The moonlight didn't pierce more than ten feet beyond the front line of trees.

The forest was quiet. This time of year the insects and wildlife wouldn't be making much noise, but the silence was much deeper and more imposing. The woods knew something. The snapping of another branch, which sounded much thicker, echoed through the forest with a juxtaposed intensity.

Barry bolted upright, simultaneously coughing out smoke, stuffing the baggy into his pocket, and hiding the smoldering bubbler behind him. He faced the woods and waited for whoever was out there to come forward. There was no movement. He squinted as he peered through the darkness, searching the trees for the source of the noise. His heart nearly leapt out of his throat when he found it.

A tall, wide-shouldered man was standing in the darkness, partially obstructed by a tree, staring at him. The man was easily six foot nine and was wider than a refrigerator. The behemoth wasn't fat either; he seemed thick with muscle. He stood quietly, patiently eyeing Barry with his hand limp at his side. What was most startling was the fact that the man had no facial features. A cold, black mask blended with the shadows and removed any trace of humanity.

They stared at one another for what seemed like an eternity to Barry. He was paralyzed with fear. He didn't want to make a move that would set the beast in motion. He didn't have to.

The hulk stepped out into full view and Barry saw that, in his other hand, which had been blocked by the tree, was a large hunting knife. The man broke into a charge and rushed through the tree line toward him.

Barry didn't know if the man was going to scale the fence or plow through it, but he didn't want to wait to find out. Abandoning the bubbler on the Lincoln, he jumped off the hood and stumbled when he hit the dirt. Quickly regaining his balance, he took off into the junkyard in the direction of the Beck's front office. He weaved through piles of mufflers, kitchen appliances, entire ovens, and junk from the tri-county area. His legs obediently carried him toward the official entrance of the yard. He couldn't afford to be still. He glanced over his shoulder for any sign of the man: nothing but rusted pickups and old washing machines. The junkyard was as lifeless as always.

He stopped momentarily to look for the light that stayed lit on the back of the trailer that served as a front office. He had set off in the general direction of the entrance but had twisted and turned along the bolt and nail ridden paths so many times he needed to get his bearings.

A coughing fit seized him as he looked around. Damning the smoke he had recently inhaled, he ran again before the man could locate the source of the coughs. When he rounded a particularly rust-laden pile of junk, the trailer office came in to view. What he didn't see was the mountainous man lurking behind an old Ford resting on its axles.

At first, the steel rod didn't hurt when it impaled Barry through his back, puncturing through a kidney and intestines before it exited near his belly button. The initial few milliseconds were simply shock. His nerve endings sent impulses screaming to his brain immediately thereafter. The man lifted Barry with the rod and the pain became blinding. Barry cried out and shouted for help. He was too far from the school for anyone at the dance to hear, and chances were neither Beck brother was still in the office as late as it was.

With the sounds of Barry's anguish the monstrosity heaved him backwards into the excessively rusty pile of scrap. The wound stretched and ripped larger, allowing blood to ooze out. His punctured intestine also seemed to try and squeeze out. On impact with the rusty pile, sharp edges cut his flesh in various places on his back, arms, and legs. The impact also knocked the wind out of him and pushed the rod almost completely through. He cried out again. The man closed in once more.

As the man slowly approached him, Barry knew he had to pull the steel rod out so he could run, or face certain death. He planted his feet on the ground at the base of the pile and, as he stood, he gripped the steel with two hands and pulled it completely out. Screaming both in pain and with adrenaline, he swung the rod with all his might and smacked the beast in the head. The hit landed with a crunch. He hoped it was the man's skull.

The masked face turned back to him after the hit. There was blood trickling out of one ear, but he seemed otherwise unfazed. The mask was cracked, but most of the force had hit right at the ear and behind. The blood that was seeping out appeared black in the night.

Barry's blood still seemed bright red as it pooled in the hand he had clutched at his stomach. He dropped the steel rod and moved as quickly as he could back toward the secret hole in the fence. His run was more of a half-bent scurry. He couldn't stand straight.

The man walked patiently behind him, kept pace, and waited for his prey to succumb to the wound.

When the fence came into view, Barry saw that the man had not gone over the fence but through it. The opening in the tall chain link that Barry had originally squeezed through had been ripped and peeled back into a gaping hole. He didn't want to think about the strength the feat required. He made it through and ignored the pain. He screamed toward the school for help as he reached the football field, but everyone had gone inside where music was blaring. The shouting aggravated his wound and sent pain reverberating through his body. He collapsed and fell to his knees less than halfway across the field.

The black-masked face appeared once more. The grizzly man stood before him and raised the steel rod above his head.

Things began to blur and swirl for Barry. The pain was dizzying and the blood loss drained him. He looked up, still clutching his stomach, and watched as the massive man swung the rod. He thought he heard a grunt from under the mask just before the rod crushed down and things went black.

Chapter 16

The night passed in a hazy tumult. Rook tossed and turned, trying to sleep so he could confront Apxutaraxi. Whether it was shock, guilt, fear, or Apxutaraxi himself fighting, Rook could not find sleep. He was left with his thoughts.

He could see the knife sliding into Jon's throat and feel the resistance in the blade as Apxutaraxi slid it through. The life flickered out of Jon's eyes over and over again. He saw serpents behind his own eyes when he closed them. Great, black snakes writhed en masse. He tried to look past them, to the veil of dreams, into his subconscious. They hissed and struck out at him, impossibly long fangs dripping with venom. Apxutaraxi didn't want to play, it seemed.

Lying in bed, sweating through the sheets despite the cool outside air he was letting in, he turned once more onto his back. His arm burned as if he had massaged poison ivy into it. He scratched it profusely, unable to stay the itch. The black veins had spread from the back of his hand and extended up just past the elbow. He had a feeling that, once they crept past his shoulder and reached his heart, they would explode through the rest of his body. The skin on his arm was red and blotchy. He had scratched hard enough to make trails of pinpoint blood. As he examined the damage, the veins in his arm moved.

It was as if they weren't his veins, but instead, the very snakes that had blocked his dreams. He screamed in horror and pain and clamped his good hand hard around the arm, above the elbow, as if to tourniquet and cut off the life below. The veins seemed angered and pushed outward in an effort to break through the skin. He saw the bulge of a snake's head just below his elbow and blacked out.

***

When he opened his eyes again, it was morning. Tank was sitting at the side of the bed, facing him, snout rested on the mattress. Either he had to pee or he was concerned, or both. Rook couldn't decide.

He sat up and the blanket fell from his chest, blasting him with icy air that had filled the room after he blacked out with the window open. He checked his arm. No sign of snakes burrowing through his flesh, but the veins were black and reached just above his elbow as they had during the night. Sure, he'd be called crazy if he told Dr. Harper about what Apxutaraxi had done, well crazier, but how would the doctor explain the black veins? It sure as hell wasn't vitamin deficiency.

He swung his legs over the edge of the bed and touched his feet to the floor. Tank nudged his legs anxiously with his massive head and then looked up at him with big, brown eyes.

He did know something was wrong.

"You want to go outside, boy?"

And he did have to pee.

Tank clawed at the door, as he had been told not to numerous times before.

Rook closed his window and then popped the front door open long enough for Tank to slip out. More cold air gushed in. The forecasters were right; there was ice headed toward Kyruht.

No plan had come to him as he'd hoped it would. He had killed a good man who was a good friend, and he was harboring some sort of evil he hadn't the slightest idea how to destroy, if that was even possible. Jon had said the evil couldn't be destroyed, only contained, and Apxutaraxi had seen to it Rook wouldn't learn how to contain him. Every way he looked at it, his life as he knew it was over. No more would he be able to hide away in his cozy little cabin with Tank. Even if he wasn't found out by the police, Apxutaraxi would certainly continue taking control and doing unthinkable things.

The only course of action that occurred to him was a risky and most likely foolish one. He would go to Jon's shop and hope to God that he could find something useful there, a magically endowed dream catcher or a blessed, sacred arrow or even just a tidbit of useful information. Searching the shop would require breaking and entering, but he didn't want to go back to Jon's house and risk another trap. Loitering around the scene of the crime would be bad enough, let alone if he got stuck there. He just hoped he wouldn't be walking directly into the waiting arms of the police if he drove into town.

***

Tank stood, then sat, then stood, then sat, then stood again. He was always anxious when he had to ride in front. Rook wasn't about to let him ride in the bed when the wind whipping around the truck was flirting with freezing point and bits of ice were falling from the sky. The forecasters had called for the storm to impact the area the next day, but it seemed the gloomy skies didn't want to wait. They instead gave a preview of what was to come.

The ice pellets continued to clink softly off his windshield as he slowed coming into town. Nothing seemed out of the normal yet. There were no road-blocks and flashing cherries to greet him. It was odd, however, seeing Shelby's Diner packed full. Every parking spot was occupied. A few bold patrons ventured to park on the median between the lot and the highway.

He didn't want to know why the town was cramming into the diner, and he was going to drive directly to the police station for some business when Dawn spotted him. He hadn't noticed her smoking beside the diner until she waved him over, without her usual smile.

One arm, with cigarette in hand, waved him toward her direction while the other stayed wrapped around her coat in an effort to stay warm. The fuzzy fur hood to her coat was at her neck, leaving her face exposed to the breezes that managed to wrap around to her side of the building. Her cheeks were white, but not as pale as the shivering legs left exposed by her work skirt.

Rook raised a hand to his window to acknowledge her and turned into the lot. The whole town wouldn't have gathered together to arrest him. Something else was going on. If it was indeed a how-to-handle-Rook meeting, it would save him the trip to the police station. He had planned to take Tank to the station simultaneously to keep up appearances, make sure Tank had a warm place to stay if he did get arrested, and check in on what they knew.

Dawn didn't wait for him to park. Cold, she hurried back inside. He watched her scamper and resolved to park near the front door, blocking several other cars that had actually found spots.

He turned to Tank and petted him on the head. "Sit tight, bud. I'll be right back." He thought about it a moment. "Well, someone will be right back for you."

He left the truck running with the heat on low and hopped out. Inside the diner the chatter was deafening. Mr. Renelette had a half-dozen people crammed into his booth, listening intently as he spun tales. Another two dozen people stood in groups, buzzing. He listened to the closest group, consisting of Mrs. Fuhrman, the principal of the school, and two other teachers:

"Can you believe it?"

"The poor dear!"

"Who would do such a thing?"

"They found him covered in blood . . ."

Rook's gut tightened and did flips.

"Rook!"

His name cut through the air and sent an icy bolt up his spine.

"Hey, Rook! Over here!" Dawn was on the other side of the main counter with the staff. Miles and Mike sat on the patron side of the counter, talking with them.

He hadn't been jumped with handcuffs yet. He gulped and walked to Dawn's group. Her Shelby's coworkers peeled off, leaving Rook with the Distance gang.

"Did you hear what happened?!"She looked at him earnestly. Her eyes were puffy and red. He hadn't noticed when in the truck, but she had been crying.

through the lot. He didn't hit any cars on his straight path through, but he did hop the curb at the end of the parking lot and pin the truck in a ditch. Either the people in the diner were so preoccupied with tales of Barry they didn't see the truck, or they simply didn't realize it was a dog driving away.

"Jesus, Tank!" He ran to the truck and nearly slipped on the thin layer of ice that had formed on the pavement. The skies had let up for the time being, though.

From behind him he heard Tatum call out, "He's okay! I looked before I came in to get you."

He slid a few feet down into the ditch alongside the truck, still puffing exhaust out of its tail pipe. His breath frosted against the window as he looked in through the driver's side. Tank looked up at him, blissfully unaware of the trouble he had created with an errant tail wag, his tail still wagging.

Rook couldn't help but chuckle looking into those big, brown eyes. He pulled open the door and vigorously roughed up Tank's fur with both hands. "I hope you know I'm leashing you to this truck and making you pull it out." He kissed Tank on the head.

"May as well turn it off. There's no way we're getting it out of there now. I'll have the Becks tow you out once we clear them." Tatum stood at the top of the ditch, looking down. For the first time he looked like a real officer of the law to Rook. His hands were on his waist, along with his belt holding his firearm, cuffs, mace, and baton. He'd only ever used the cuffs in Kyruht. There was never a need for weaponry outside the firing range. His brown shirt, tucked into his light brown pants, and brown hat contrasted greatly against the light gray sky behind him. He'd never been so imposing before.

Tatum extended a hand as Rook climbed up the side of the ditch slick with ice. Tank made the hill easily on all fours.

"Hop into the car," Tatum told him.

Rook hadn't planned on voluntarily getting into a police car when he formed the idea to break into the pawnshop. It was against his every instinct.

"It's okay, Tate. I'll walk Tank over to the station and then run a few errands while I wait for the Becks."

"Nonsense, I'm going over there anyway. It's a short walk, but why bother? Just put Tank in the back."

And so, after placing Tank in the backseat like a criminal, Rook climbed into the car that would soon enough be chasing after him. He looked back to see Tank and found that the lab was already seated, looking directly at him with his nose squished against the dividing glass. Warm air blasted out of the vents against his arms and legs, and "Sad Songs" belted out through the radio.

He looked at Tatum without saying a word.

"Don't give me that look. Elton John is the man." Tatum threw the car in gear.

No sooner had he shifted gears when Rose's voice came through on the CB. "Bobby, you read?"

Tatum quieted Elton John, picked up the mic, and gave an affirmative response.

Rose buzzed through again, "Don't bother coming back. Sue isn't done yet and you got a job to do."

"Copy that, Rose. What do you have in mind?" Tatum's foot stayed flat on the brake, his left hand on the wheel, waiting to turn.

"Jon never opened up the shop this morning and he hasn't answered any calls. Can you go on by his place and make sure everything's all right?"

Rook's heart ceased pumping and climbed into his throat, securely above his voice box.

"Yeah. No problem. Over and out." Tatum clunked the mic back into its holster. "You want to go say hi to Jon real quick?" He looked over at Rook inquiringly.

Oh, yeah, sure, we can even have a drink with him, he thought bitterly to himself. Guilt, grief, and anger bubbled up inside him like agitated froth. Although, he continued thinking, he could tag along and guide Tatum's search, providing errant speculations and planting ideas to throw Kyruht's finest off. Or, if necessary, he could stop Tatum entirely.

He was plotting against his friend to conceal the

murder of another friend. Even without Apxutaraxi in control, he was more nefarious than ever. He could see things spinning out of control down a dark corridor without return. He had never been a malicious man, even in the wake of the atrocities he had survived. He wouldn't become as malevolent as *him*. He would never be like *him* in any regard. And yet, there he sat, contemplating ways to conceal murder at the cost of his still-living friends. Was it Apxutaraxi or was it that part of him he wished didn't exist?

Tatum could see he was thinking; he just had no idea the depths to which those thoughts extended. "C'mon. Whatever errands you have can wait. We'll go see what the old man is up to and have a quick drink with him. He's probably sloshed or hungover. I ran into him at the store the other day and he told me he was brewing something special." He cast a mischievous smile rife with want for drink.

Rook's heart slid back out of his throat and started pounding. Just how much had Jon told Tatum? He had to know.

He made a rash decision.

His voice tried to tremble, but he played it off as a clearing of the throat. "A drink would be great."

The words sounded genuine as he forced them out. They were half-honest. A drink, or a dozen, would've been amazing.

Tatum eased off the brake, turned onto the highway, and reached for the mic one more time. "Hey, Rose. Rook is tagging along with me. He's gonna need a tow once Sheriff Wzorek is done with the Becks."

With that he hung the mic once more and brought Elton John back to a comfortable volume level. The drive was mostly void of conversation, except for when Rook asked if Jon had said anything about the liquor he was mixing. Apparently he hadn't given much more than a "Hey, how ya doin'? What are you up to?" when they bumped into each other.

As they pulled into the long driveway that led to Jon's house, Tatum flicked the windshield wipers on for a second to clear the little ice that had collected and Elton John wanted to slaughter a fatted calf for Bennie and the Jets.

A fatted calf . . . Kind of like that fat bastard in the back room, eh, Rookie?

Apxutaraxi. Not only Apxutaraxi. He was after the fat man again.

"You all right, Rook?" Tatum asked.

"Uh, yeah. Why?" He sniffled.

"Because your nose is bleeding and you're breathing like you just ran a 10k."

He felt more like he had been hit by a freight train. Apxutaraxi was definitely fighting to poke his ugly head out. It wouldn't be so easy this time. Rook knew what Apxutaraxi was capable of and wouldn't be caught off-guard. With Jon he had flipped like a switch. Not this time. He knew it would come again and he would concentrate to keep Apxutaraxi caged. He had to.

"Dry air. You got any tissues in here?" He cupped his hand under his nose. It wasn't a gusher, but blood was indeed seeping out.

Tatum reached in front of him and pulled a small pouch of tissue paper out of the glove box. "Stop that nose up. I don't want blood all over my seats. We'll see if Jon can fix you up with a rag to hold under that thing in a minute."

I highly doubt the Injun can provide any hospitality . . .

Apxutaraxi trailed off. He sounded farther away that time.

"Thanks," Rook said as he pinched the tissue under his nose and tilted his head.

The lights in Jon's house were still ablaze. His gray Ford F-150 sat cold and dotted with ice. The front door was open.

When Apxutaraxi had tried to leave, he got the front door open before Jon's trap stopped him at the threshold. Rook never had been able to go farther. He could have reached through the flames and grabbed the doorknob to pull it shut, but the thought hadn't occurred to him. The only thing on his mind at the point was the pain.

"Something's not right." Tatum snapped into form. "Wait here."

He parked the car in the narrow of the driveway just behind the truck. No suspects of malintent would be able to hop into Jon's truck and make a quick getaway without having to pull forward and make some sort of Austin Powers attempt to turn around between the house and the car. Of course, Tatum didn't know he had the murderer in his vehicle already.

He exited the vehicle and walked around the truck toward the front door. As he walked, he unbuttoned his holster and withdrew his firearm.

"Jon!?" he shouted into the home as he stepped over the line that had trapped Rook.

Rook wouldn't wait in the car. He had to mislead Tatum as he uncovered the scene and his mind was buzzing. He could walk right in but would have to exit through the hole in the wall again. It would be easy enough to play detective with Tatum and step back outside through the hole in search of a trail he was certain he didn't leave.

Hesitating briefly at the line, he stepped back in to Jon's house. "Tate? Jon?" *Nice touch*, he thought, calling *for Jon as well*. "You all right?"

"In here," he heard Tatum say from the room where Jon's body was lying.

Seeing Jon's body again would elicit genuine grief; he wouldn't have to act on that one. When he entered the room, however, he was met with genuine surprise. The carpet was stained with blood, but the body and the sheet he'd draped were gone.

"What is going on here?" Tatum said in dismay and frustration "First the hikers, then Barry, and now this?" He motioned to the blood.

Dead men don't walk, but Rook still felt himself ask the question, "Do you think Jon is all right?" His head was swimming. Jon had been dead; he was sure of it. It was a terrible thought, but animals had to have dragged the carcass off. Jon wasn't out on the town.

Tatum hesitated and sighed. "I don't know, but that's a lot of blood. If it's his, he's definitely in trouble."

I'll keep asking the dumb questions, Rook decided. "What do you think happened?"

"Hard to tell, but it looks like there was a struggle. The table and chairs are disheveled." Rook's chair was indeed knocked over. "And something else was spilled on the carpet over there." Tatum did have a good eye for detail.

Rook pretended to examine the scene with Tatum, who was especially drawn by the gaping hole in the wall.

"What did you think about the Benedict guy that was in the tank the other day?" *Think about Benedict, the mildly aggressive drunk who threatens dogs. He's an imposing-looking man, a stranger, an unknown. He could have brought trouble when he drifted into town, if it was just a happenstance drift and not deliberate malfeasance from the beginning.* Rook got the wheels turning in Tatum's head, or he hoped he had.

Benedict seemed to be a harmless drunk. It probably wasn't him who beat the hell out of Barry and it certainly wasn't he who killed Jon, if Jon was actually killed. Rook considered Benedict. He had known about the black veins, but that could have very easily been Apxutaraxi twisting Rook's mind into thinking Benedict was talking.

"Benedict?" Tatum questioned. "He was just a drunk."

"I mean, do you think he could be behind any of this? Who else in town could you even imagine attacking Barry or Jon?"

"But why would he? They both look like very deliberate attacks. Barry was walking around alone and Jon was out here. They couldn't have provoked him into a crime in the heat of the moment. Besides, he had a wad of cash and that Geo. He wouldn't need to kill them to acquire anything he didn't already have."

"How do you think he got that wad of cash?" Rook played his cards carefully and led Tatum down the path to suspect number one. Benedict certainly hadn't obtained so much money by asking people nicely and that thought could persuade Tatum to look into him.

"Not a bad question, Rook. What I want to know, though, is why someone would go through the trouble of breaking through the wall to get out? I mean, look at the siding here." He moved his fingers around the edge of the siding. "It's pushed outward. Somebody broke through the wall of the house to get *out.*" He emphasized the word. "And why is there dirt in front of all of the doors?"

He had been much more observant than Rook gave him credit for, too observant.

Kill him.

"What about that other hiker?"

"Rudy Bustwick. He is a suspect until he turns up."

"Rudy," Rook said to himself. The name resonated for some reason.

"I'd better get this called in. Why don't you come on back to the car?" Tatum ushered him toward the front door. "We don't want to contaminate the scene any more than we already have."

Kill him.

Rook couldn't go through the front door. He had to go through the wall. He had to think fast. Hesitation or resistance would only serve to draw Tatum's attention.

"What is that?" He focused his eyes through the hole in the wall and nodded.

"What?" Tatum didn't see the imaginary object.

"That right there. It looks like a . . . a knife or something." Rook carefully stepped and squeezed though the hole as he had before.

"Whoa, whoa, whoa, don't touch anything!" Tatum shouted after him

He took a few steps, pretended to look toward the ground, and then turned around to Tatum, who was climbing out. "I guess I was seeing things. There's nothing here."

Tatum was utterly defenseless as he clambered out. He was taller than Rook, which made the fit difficult. His long torso prohibited him from first stepping through. He had to go headfirst, one arm out to brace and one pinned at his side.

Pick up that rock and bash his head in! KILL HIM!

Apxutaraxi's intentions were clear, but he was

unable to do his own dirty work. Rook had a solid hold on him. Although, it really would be easy to pick up that rock, ten pounds at most, and swing the jagged edge toward the back of Tatum's skull as he squeezed out. The rock would feel delightfully heavy in his hands. No. No, it was Apxutaraxi thinking those things. He wasn't even speaking but thinking those things. Apxutaraxi was deeper rooted than before.

"Get out," Rook said under his breath.

"I would if you'd lend me a hand here," Tatum replied. Apparently the words hadn't been as mumbled as Rook intended. "My jacket snagged on the siding."

Do it! Kill him!

Rook moved toward Tatum and the house. He bent to pick up the rock and hoisted it up. It was even heavier than he'd guessed. It had to be close to twenty pounds of bone-crushing stone. He held the rock above Tatum's head.

"What the hell are you doing?!"Tatum shrieked.

"Put your hand on this. You can hold yourself up higher and not rub against the siding that way."

Rook placed the rock directly beneath Tatum, who did as he was instructed. Rook reached under his belly and found the snag.

"I thought you were going to smash my head with that thing!" Tatum exclaimed as he stood.

Rook laughed. "Why would I do that?"

"I don't know, but you had me scared!" Tatum didn't take his eyes off of him. "You could've told me what you were going to do."

"I did." Rook smiled.

"Yeah, only after you had the rock over my head! Jesus." Tatum laughed. "Get in the car, you psycho."

Rook felt blood trickle down his nose again.

He has no idea . . .

Chapter 17

Sheriff Wzorek paced back and forth in her office, speaking loudly. Tatum stood tall and erect, frozen and silent. Rook couldn't make out what was being said, but Tatum was clearly in trouble, probably for taking Rook to a crime scene, and thusly contaminating it. If they did find any evidence linking Rook to the scene, he could say it happened when he went through with Tatum. Apxutaraxi lucked out; he lucked out.

Sheriff Wzorek, or Sue, as Rose called her, was a petite woman with short, blond hair and piercing, green eyes that would make even the hardest deputy cower. Sheriff Wzorek was petite only until you got to know her. Then she was the biggest, toughest woman you'd ever met. Through hard work and determination she rose up through the ranks in Portland, notably surviving a shootout with three gunmen in which she fatally wounded one of the suspects. After her conduct in the incident was cleared, she applied for a position outside the city and, after testing, was found qualified to be sheriff in Kyruht. Whether it was because she had killed a man or because she simply demanded it, she had the respect of everyone in the town.

After the incident with his parents, Rook was bumped around not only homes but schools quite a bit. He never became attached or made many friends. He was a troublemaker for those first few years. In fifth grade he brought a knife to school one day. Not to hurt anyone, but to show Justin Thomas. Justin was a fellow misguided youth with an abusive father. Although he never told Justin everything, he did share enough to prove to Justin that they were kindred spirits.

The knife was a switchblade with a jade holster

displaying an elaborately outlined eagle. It had belonged to Rook's biological "father." He didn't want to remember the monster. If he had things his way, all traces of the man's existence would be wiped from the face of the earth. The knife was a symbol, though, a symbol of defiance. He had been warned not to touch it; the penalty was high, and yet he swiped it. He didn't particularly want the knife. He just wanted to defy his "father." He cringed even thinking that word. The first time child protective services stepped in, he grabbed the knife as he was hurried out with his belongings. After his second foray with child protective services, he kept the knife as a reminder of what he had overcome and the strength he needed.

The day he brought the knife to school, he pulled it out of his pocket at recess.

"Wow! Can I hold it?"

Justin was immediately smitten with the knife. He reached for it, but Rook pulled back his hands.

"No. It's just to look at." He flipped open the blade. "See. It's cool, isn't it?"

Justin reached again. "C'mon, man. I'm not gonna break it. I just want to get a better look."

"I said no."

If it weren't for the fact that he was holding a lethal object in his hand, the squabble would have been like any other bickering between friends. Before he could register what had happened, he was sitting outside the principal's office listening to Justin tell his side of the story with a gauze-wrapped hand. Justin maintained that Rook got angry and deliberately swiped at him. He put up his hand reflexively and sustained the gash to his palm. As Rook remembered it, Justin had become too aggressive and tried to force the knife out of his hands. Rook tugged back and the blade sliced open Justin's hand just below the wrist. The principal didn't believe him, though. He was expelled and forced to resume seeing a psychiatrist. A few summer classes and he was back on track, at a different school, by the next school year.

Sitting outside Sheriff Wzorek's office, he felt like

he was about to speak to the principal again. The door opened and Tatum stepped out.

"I won't be letting you tag along again!" He gave a wide-eyed grin and chuckled.

"Sorry, man. I didn't mean to get you in trouble."

"Nah, it's cool. I'm not the only one in trouble."

Sheriff Wzorek's voice commanded Rook into the office. "Can I talk to you for a second please?" She motioned him in through the door.

Tatum wished him luck and quickly disappeared.

He stepped from the lion's den directly into the mouth of the lion.

"Have a seat. I want to ask you a few questions. Oh, and the Becks went to get their tow truck. They'll have your truck out in a few minutes."

He didn't say anything. He didn't know what to say.

She stared at him for a moment. "First of all, turn off the truck. Next time Tank might not be so lucky."

"I know. I'm sorry about that. I was just running in to the diner for a second to see what the commotion was. I didn't think . . ."

She cut him off with a wave of her hand. "It's okay. I'm more upset with Bobby. I mean, Deputy Tatum. He shouldn't have brought you along."

The ice pellets had turned to freezing rain and were streaking down the giant window behind her. Rook wondered if she and Tatum really did have something going on beyond his puppy-like infatuation. It wasn't like her to refer to a deputy by his first name.

"I'll jump out of the car next time." He crossed his heart and smiled. "Promise."

"Thank you. Now I want to ask you about Jon. If you feel you need a lawyer present, that's fine. We can stop and make the questioning more formal."

"Questioning? A lawyer? Jesus, Sheriff. Am I a suspect?"

"No one is a suspect," she assured him. "I just wanted to ask you about the fight at Jon's shop the other day."

How did she know about the ruckus? "Fight?"

"Mr. Renelette said he saw you leaving Jon's shop in a hurry and Mrs. Kuhrzman, who had been walking nearby, said she heard Jon shouting. I dismissed their reports at the time, but now that Jon is missing, I have to ask."

"That? That wasn't a fight. I brought in this carving I found when I was hiking and he got all bent out of shape about it. He didn't want the thing anywhere near his shop. Something superstitious, I guess. He called to apologize for it later."

She studied him with her ferociously green eyes. "He threw you out of his shop because of a carving?"

"I guess so. Something else must have had him stressed out." He was getting good at misdirection.

"Would you mind showing me this carving?"

Something in him hated the idea. Apxutaraxi didn't want to lose the wolf. They were definitely connected. He ran through the event at Jon's in his mind and made sure he hadn't left anything incriminating with the carving after he tucked it away in his truck. "It's actually in my glove-box right now."

"Do you mind if we take a look at it?"

Yes.

"Not at all." He could feel Apxutaraxi becoming aggravated and took enjoyment out of poking the sleeping bear. "It should probably be in a museum or something anyway. It's all yours."

Sue expressed her gratitude. "Thank you. I'll make sure it's properly handled."

"So you thought I would need a lawyer for that?"

"You never know." She smiled but didn't take her eyes off of him. Like a well-trained bloodhound, she could smell something was up. She wasn't sure what yet, but she was picking up a trail to something big.

Something, something, something is creeping up. Something is building. Something IS going to happen.

Apxutaraxi was increasingly restless. It hadn't taken long for him to regain strength after what happened at Jon's, not with Rook boldly goading him.

Rook sniffled. "Is it okay if I go now?" He could feel blood trying to run out of his nose and a maelstrom of a headache was winding up. He couldn't afford to be sucked away into la-la land.

"Sure. Be careful out there. It's supposed to get nasty." She examined him once more, continuing to search for truth she was certain was hidden.

He hadn't even said anything incriminating and still she was onto him. The years had finely tuned her senses, he supposed. "Before I go, do you have any ibuprofen? My head is killing me."

The sheriff pulled a small bottle out of her desk and tossed it to him. "Keep it."

"Thanks." He smiled at her for the last time.

Chapter 18

Mike hated Miles for bailing, was mad at Dawn for not covering, and hated Distance Grocery for existing. He bet Miles's parents thought they were cute and clever for naming their boy Miles Distance. He wanted to punch each of them square in the face.

Mike tossed the mop into its bucket and kicked the pale on wheels to the other end of the aisle. He would dump the mop water when he went to the backroom. The equally mind-numbing task of restocking crackers awaited him first.

Distance was already short-staffed, and with Barry's coma, the crew was smaller than ever. He wanted to see Barry up at the hospital, but Mike couldn't get out of his shift. Miles didn't give a rat's ass about Barry. He was only worried about himself and how he could continue to dodge work with an even shorter staff.

Miles, the manager and golden-boy son of Mr. Distance himself, was supposed to be there alongside Mike, but decided he didn't want to work. Mike figured he had disappeared into his office to play the Xbox he had set up there. He wondered if Mr. Distance knew about the Xbox. Even if he did, he wouldn't make Miles remove it.

Finally, Mike's frustration broke him. "Fuck this place." Shouting toward the east side of the building where Miles's office was located, he continued, "You're on your own, Miles! Fuck you, and fuck this shitty job! I'll get a job at Bender's and make twice as much bartending there! Plus I'll get time off to see my best friend, who's in a *coma!*"

Amazed by his own outburst, Mike waited patiently

for any indication that Miles had heard him. Silence filled the store like a balloon. Mike waited for the pop. Nothing.

The store remained poised in quiet. The fluorescent lights overhead flickered for a moment, not uncommon for Mike. He had worked many nights.

"You hear me, Miles?!"

There was no response. He tore his Distance Grocery apron off and tossed it to the ground. He walked to the end of the aisle near the registers and turned the corner toward Miles's office. The lights weren't on. Miles was probably sleeping.

Mike muttered under his breath, "Fucking figures." He waited for a response for a few seconds longer. "Damn it, Miles, answer me! I'm really quitting this time!"

Out of his peripheral he saw a large, dirty fist closing in. It was too late. The hit landed on his temple and dropped him immediately to the ground. In the eight seconds he was unconscious the killer picked him up by the shoulders and stood him face to face. The killer studied Mike as his eyes flitted back open and adjusted.

An angry black mask was all that was before him. Its hard surface was scarred with scratches gouged further by the overhead light. The mask was cracked on the left side and dried blood matted the hair and ear of whoever was behind it. There was no mouth, only slanted, narrowed eyes with a furrow between them. There was an undying, concentrated rage in those eyes. Mike struggled to see human eyes behind the mask, but only darkness dwelled in the sockets. The man's neck was nearly nonexistent and his oversized trapezius muscles had black veins the size of garden hoses.

He summoned his strength to struggle, but the creature held firm. It was no man. Mike came to this realization as he looked into the empty sockets. Lacking rationale, with only anger as a guide, man was no more than a beast.

The beast's fingers dug deeply into Mike's shoulders. At any moment the bones would snap. The pressure was excruciating. He screamed for help. The beast released Mike's shoulders and grabbed his neck with a single hand. As it lifted him off his feet, Mike gasped for air. His trachea felt crushed flat. The beast didn't hold him for long and instead hurled him against an aisle end display. The vertebrae in his back cracked on impact with the metal shelves. Cheese puffs and tortilla chips went flying. The beast tore a candy rack off of another shelf and hurled it in his direction. Chocolate bars bounced and skidded across the floor.

Mike's lungs burned and his head throbbed. He crawled toward the office, but the beast stepped in front of him with a large hunting knife in hand. The knife was then plunged high into the soft corkboard in the shelving where he had just crashed. The beast grabbed at him with cinderblock hands that crushed and knocked the wind out of him like a bear viciously batting at its victim. The paws eventually clamped onto his flailing, pain-riddled body and hoisted him into the air once more. He was slammed against the same steel shelves behind where the corkboard and knife waited. With one gargantuan hand around Mike's throat, the beast held him in place and withdrew the blade.

In an instinctive, last-ditch effort, Mike threw his arm up defensively in front of him. The beast sliced deep into the meat of his arm and he recoiled in pain. Another scream escaped. Blood poured out of the wound and formed a puddle at his feet as quickly as the beast cocked back for a second swing. Mike swung wildly at the masked murderer and, despite a solid connection under the chin on the behemoth, the knife plunged again. Mike gasped and choked on blood as the blade slid between his ribs and pierced his lung. Bloody spittle sprayed out of his mouth with his final breaths. The beast slammed the knife through him savagely. The large knife slid effortlessly through his flesh over and over, scraping bones and cleaving organs.

Half-asleep, he ignored Mike's rant, but Miles nearly fell out of his chair when he heard a scream. He had been snoozing peacefully in the dark with his feet on his desk. He groggily rubbed his eyes and muttered about Mike messing around. When he heard the second, blood-curdling scream, he jumped to full attention. What he heard wasn't horseplay.

Stammering out of the office, he called out to the aisles, "Mike! Are you okay?!"A can fell to the ground with a clank a few aisles over. He went toward the front and was assaulted with fear when he saw Mike's limp, butchered body lying in a heap, surrounded by a puddle of blood-saturated chips.

"Oh God, oh God, oh God." His bowels trembled and he felt a familiar warmth trickling down his leg and soaking into his sock. He turned and ran toward the office, immediately slammed the door shut behind him, and locked it. Peering between the blinds in his window, he checked to see if anyone followed behind him. The store was quiet and the few fluorescents that were on did their usual dance. He scuttled on all fours under his desk and pulled the office phone down with him. He dialed 911, but the phone beeped the "not allowed" tone.

"Goddamn it! There are three phones in this fucking store. I shouldn't have to bother dialing nine to get out!" Frantically he punched the nine and the first two digits, but the window exploded into the office, startling the phone dock out of his hand. It hit the floor and disconnected. Mike's mangled carcass smashed against the wooden desk with bits of glass. His cold, lifeless eyes met Miles's. "Holy shit!" Miles screamed and clambered for the phone, but a massive boot slammed down on his hand, breaking three of his fingers. The crunching and snapping of the bones seemed to echo louder than his cry of agony.

Out of the corner of his eye he saw the glimmer of a nine-inch letter opener that had fallen from his desk in the crash. He grabbed it with his free hand and stabbed through the foot. He gambled that, as he stabbed, the man would let up enough for him to remove his twisted digits before the blade impaled them both. His gamble failed, but all was not lost. He didn't stab his hand; the cool metal of the blade rested between his fingers.

Roaring with anger, the brute tore his foot from the ground and flipped the desk with complete disregard to the weight of the heavy wood. Miles didn't waste a second retrieving his hand and jumped over the upturned desk toward the door while the brute pulled the letter opener out. He tugged at the door with every ounce of strength, but it was still locked. The killer had come through the window. He fumbled at the lock and turned the knob as soon as it clicked. Before he could pull, the beast charged forward and shoved the letter opener through the back of his head, simultaneously skewering his brain and pinning him to the door.

Miles wasn't immediately killed. The blade had paralyzed him from the neck down and deflated his right eye, but his heart remained beating. Damaged signals made him irrepressibly sing the Oscar Meyer Weiner song, but his vocal cords did not respond appropriately, so it came out as a gargled whisper. He closed his remaining eye and was gone to summer camp when he was a little boy. He and his friends were throwing rocks into an algae-covered pond, trying to hit bullfrogs. When he did hit one and saw it fall limp just below the surface of the water, he wanted to cry. The helpless creature lay there dead, after having been hopping along merrily moments before. With a dull thud, the brute's hunting knife severed Miles's head and his body fell to the floor.

Chapter 19

That night, Rook decided on what would prove to be a very costly mistake. He couldn't face another night in the dark with Apxutaraxi, not when Apxutaraxi had seemingly regained his strength. Unable to close his eyes for fear of being pulled in, Rook resolved himself to breaking and entering. He was back to his original plan of searching Jon's shop for any shred of useful information.

He wouldn't be able to drop Tank off at the station before his crime spree this time, so he prepared for the worst. Rook left Tank's kibble bag within the dog's reach so he could tear it open if his food bowl was empty for too long. Rook also left the toilet seat up so Tank could drink out of it in the event his old five-quart ice cream container ran dry. It wasn't the most elegant solution, but it would do.

"Here, boy." Rook patted his thighs.

Tank obediently trotted over with his head hung low and tail between his legs.

"It's okay, buddy. You'll be all right." He hooked his thumbs over Tank's ears and scratched behind them with his fingers.

Tank whimpered softly. His superior senses were sending up warning flags Rook was unable to see as a human.

"If I don't come back, someone else will be sent to get you. Then you can play every day with Duke." He reassured the dog and gave him a kiss on the head.

Tank nuzzled his cheek.

Rook walked to the door and put a stocking cap on along with his warm coat. "I love you. Now be a good boy and keep an eye on the place. No parties while I'm gone."

Before he could step out of the door, he felt a strong tug on his pants. Tank had carefully bitten the fabric and was pulling him back into the cabin. Rook hopped on one leg as he tried to keep his balance.

"Hey, knock that off!" He shook his captive leg vigorously.

Tank ignored him and instead pulled harder, sending him to the floor on his butt. All one hundred pounds of Tank was on top of him in seconds. He started to roll and push the dog off when Tank latched on to his arm, the same arm that had been bitten when he first found the wolf. Once again, it wasn't a hard bite, but Tank growled through his clenched teeth.

Rook was stupefied by the behavior and watched as Tank released his arm, licked his face, and repeated the procedure, never biting hard enough to hurt, but enough to show he meant business.

"I know." Rook used his free hand to gently grab Tank by the scruff of his neck and pull him off.

Satisfied his message had gotten across, Tank let himself be removed. He sat and stared at Rook, who was now in a seated position, eye to eye.

"That's why I have to go. I don't want to hurt you either. I can't control what's inside me." Rook didn't think twice about the depth of conversation he was having with a dog. There had always been an understanding between him and Tank that went beyond normal communication and commands. As everyone in town knew, Tank was a hell of a dog.

It was then, in their silent stare, that Rook truly realized he might never see Tank again. That moment could have been the last time he looked into the deep, brown eyes of his unconditionally loving friend. Fighting back a sudden onslaught of tears, he hugged the chocolate lab fiercely and gave the soft fur on Tank's head one last kiss.

***

Rook's headlights revealed a thin sheen of ice on the asphalt as he made his journey into town. The freezing rain had turned into a form near graupel in the night. *A fancy slush*, he thought to himself. The fancy slush was still hazardous, however. His truck briefly lost traction in a couple spots, hastening his already speeding heart.

He didn't want his truck seen at or near Jon's shop so he pulled off on a side road about a quarter-mile from town. Carefully he negotiated the truck off the side road toward the forest. Unless they were really looking, no one would be able to spot his truck in the dark. He was safe, from the one or two motorists who would pass by anyway.

The woods were entirely different from dusk to night. The sunlight that had warmly tucked in the forest like a mother putting her child to sleep on his previous hike was nonexistent. Darkness and starlight turned a once-vibrant forest into an eerie graveyard. Dead branches and fallen leaves crunched under his feet as he walked as close to the road as he could without being seen. He would follow alongside the road just deep enough in the woods where drivers wouldn't see him.

The silence also lent to the feeling that he was walking through a land of the dead. Only pelting ice and the occasional rustling of a critter in its nest reached his ears. Predators were the only creatures out at this time of night, he realized, predators and one Rook Evrett.

After about ten minutes of navigating the forest, Jon's shop came into view. Many of the buildings around town had forest leading right up to them. Jon's pawnshop, fortunately, was one of those buildings. Rook stayed in the shadows behind the building and quickly ran to the back door. If the diner were open, not even the eagle-eyed Mr. Renelette could have spotted him from his window booth.

The backdoor had one five-pin lock and no deadbolt. Rook doubted many of the buildings in town had bothered with deadbolts when they were originally built. After his childhood, he thought it prudent to learn how to pick locks. It didn't take much research before he knew how to make his own tension wrench and pick and work the pins. He read through a locksmith's training guide he found and practiced on locks at his foster parents' houses. They weren't particularly pleased.

A couple of minutes finagling and the door popped open. He slid into the pawnshop and pulled the door shut behind him. In the backroom the smell of smoke still clung to the air. Jon had smoked inside enough times for the walls to become saturated with the odor. The room was small, had an old couch, and was littered with boxes of beads, string, synthetic hides, feathers, and glue. He not only sold cheap exploitative merchandise, but he made it himself. Rook found himself thinking about the time he had hung out with Jon and put together a hundred bracelets over cold beers and talked about fishing for hours. Rook didn't get home until three in the morning. He wished he were on another late-night visit like that one.

Jon's shop was unremarkable. No sacred arrows or blessed tomahawks had been left in plain sight. No words of wisdom had been left behind for Rook to find, not even a book of Shasta history and folklore. Rook's imagination had him convinced that he'd find something useful or magical at the shop. His imagination had led him astray, again. An overactive mind led to a loose grip on reality. At this point he was hanging on by his pinky.

Everything was put away and in its place. The glass display counter was locked, the shelves were organized, the knick-knacks were stocked, and the little red light on the safe tucked discreetly under the counter blinked tauntingly. Jon's lethargic, small-town pawn business didn't bring in much money, and the novelties he sold on the side barely paid the bills. The safe wouldn't be holding much cash. It was probably used for a few high-value pieces of jewelry and maybe a personal item or two. Either way, he wasn't going to find out. There was no point in messing with the safe.

A muffled cry drifted across the room like a whisper. He spun around and knocked over a brochure display on the edge of the counter. No one else was in the room, but he knew the cry had been real. He scurried around and scooped up the brochures, fighting to balance the small cardboard display. On one of the brochures Crater Lake sparkled brilliantly blue. A

121

searing pain built behind his eyes and spread through his head like a hand squeezing his brain. He crumpled the brochure in his hand and shoved it into his pocket to retrieve the bottle of ibuprofen Wzorek had given him earlier. He struggled with the lid as waves of pain trembled through his body. Finally, his fingers managed to pop the cap off and he dumped the contents. He quickly swallowed the half-dozen pills that landed in his hand while others bounced across the counter.

"Shit!" Rook said aloud reaching for the pills. Then he collapsed on the floor, back against the counter, and placed his head between his knees. His head felt ready to split open in the same manner Carol and Richard's heads had. "What the fuck!?" He clamped his hands as tightly as he could against the sides of his head in hopes that the pressure would keep it from exploding outward.

His cursing question was actually directed toward Apxutaraxi, who he was sure was responsible. He hadn't been prone to exploding head syndrome prior to his mind's most recent tenant. His head hadn't hurt so bad since the night of the "accident," as Dr. Harper put it, over fifteen years back.

His nose began to bleed profusely. He held the fabric of his coat against his nose so he wouldn't drip all over the shop. With the flow of blood, his headache waned until he was able to stand and use his free hand to place the spilled pills back in the bottle. His little operation was a complete bust.

Another scream, this one louder than the last, reached his ears as he stepped out of the backdoor and closed it behind him. The scream came from the ether and, at the same time, was very near. He had a feeling he was being made to deliberately hear it. Rather than walk to the woods, he walked toward Shelby's and Distance. It wasn't long before he realized he wasn't simply being directed somewhere. He was being pulled.

He walked past the diner and toward the single loading bay of Distance. The bay door, which would have normally slid up, was instead bashed in and bent aside like it was made of thin aluminum. A single overhead light above the door illuminated the scene.

An excessively large man ducked his head under the metal and jumped down from the bay. His legs looked like tree trunks as they planted and caught his weight. He was a behemoth, and in addition to the familiarly luminescent black mask he was wearing, he held a large knife. His clothes were even more bloodstained than Rook's nose-soaked coat.

Feeling like he was in a Friday the 13th movie, every instinct told Rook to run, but he stayed rooted to the spot, his legs planted almost like tree trunks as well. The man behind the mask slowly walked toward him. He wanted to run as far away as possible, but an unseen force held him. The monster stopped within arm's length of him. For the longest twenty seconds of his life, Rook stared at the beast, and the beast stared back. He was close enough to see the gouges in the mask, and yet, oddly, he couldn't see eyes. The sockets were empty and black. Rook didn't need eyes on him to tell he was being assessed. Finally, the masked creature broke into stride, away from Rook, into darkness.

"Rook?"

He spun around to see Sheriff Wzorek come around the building.

"What's going on, Rook?" She looked at his blood-stained coat. Her eyes darted over his shoulder to the mangled door. "What did you do?"

He couldn't form a sentence. He didn't know what to say.

She unclasped her holster and placed a hand on her firearm.

"Whose blood is that?"

Silence.

The only sound was the pitter-patter of ice hitting the ground. It sounded like a hiss to Rook.

"You should come with me." She reached for her cuffs.

Chapter 20

Rook pressed his forehead to the cool surface of the table to which he was handcuffed. The station had one small room that they devoted to interrogation. It had been originally designed as an office, but with one modified table, courtesy of the Beck brothers, it had been repurposed. Rook thought it must have been ironic for the Beck brothers to be questioned at the table they themselves crafted. It was a heavy steel table with one bar, almost like a handle, bolted on the top, to which he had been cuffed for what seemed like hours.

Sheriff Wzorek had stayed late to work on the murder, assault, and missing person cases that had quickly piled up over the past couple days. It was close to midnight when she finally left, but in the parking lot, she heard screaming coming from Distance. She went to see what was going on and that's when she saw Rook walking behind the building.

When she entered the room, Rook lifted his head to see a very distraught looking sheriff. The color had been drained from her face and she looked as if she was going to vomit. She also had something small clenched in her right hand. The links in his cuffs jangled against the steel as he sat up.

"What's going on?" he asked.

"That's what I need you to tell me." She swallowed hard. "What were you doing out there?"

Rook decided a partial truth would be the best way to go. "I was walking through town and heard screams. When I went to see where they were coming from, a large man was leaving Distance through the bay. He was wearing a black mask and was covered in blood.

He walked toward me . . ."—Rook edited out the stare-off—". . . but fled when he heard you coming around the corner."

She studied him with her green eyes. They were dull and listless. Whatever had gone down at Distance had knocked her way off balance. "There was someone out there with you?"

The way she said "with you" implied accomplice. *Maybe I should ask for that lawyer,* he thought, then retorted quickly, "He wasn't with me. He was leaving the store and disappeared into the woods when you came. You had to have seen him."

Unfortunately, it had been too dark beyond the bay light and she hadn't seen the man. He knew it. Otherwise, she would've given chase or at the very least been more urgent with him.

"The blood . . ." She stared at the table.

Rook wasn't sure if she was asking about his coat, but he answered anyway. "I had a serious nosebleed." He pointed to his blood-caked nostrils. That had to be obvious.

She took a deep breath. "Rook." She seemed to be searching for words. "Mike and Miles are dead. They were both murdered tonight."

His heart sank into his stomach, which, in turn, wanted to vomit. He understood Wzorek's demeanor.

"The man, it had to be that man." He knew the blood-soaked man was no deli butcher at the grocery, but he didn't know Mike and Miles had been inside. "I didn't . . . I couldn't . . ."

"I don't believe you would, but . . ." She added, much to Rook's dismay, "I don't believe your story either. Tell me the truth, Rook. What were you doing out there?"

"I told you, I was walking." *In the middle of the night nowhere near my home,* he thought. "I couldn't sleep, so I was walking." There, it was kind of the truth.

"Walking where?!" The sheriff grew agitated and then sighed, clearly not taken in by his deceit. She looked at her hand and then tossed its contents on to the table. "What about this?"

It was a small white pill, an ibuprofen that had eluded him on Jon's display case. He kept silent.

"I thought to check out Jon's shop on a hunch. The backdoor was unlocked . . ."

Whoops. Apxutaraxi laughed.

". . . And I found several of these pills on the counter and floor."

Several? Rook wondered. Apparently he'd spilled a lot more than he thought.

You're sloppy, kid. You should leave everything to me . . .

His head ached softly.

"How do you explain the tools we found in your pocket?"

His pick and tension wrench.

Finally, he conceded. "I did break into Jon's shop . . ." He trailed off, unsure what reason he could possibly provide.

"Why, Rook? Where's Jon? What is going on?" She was bursting with questions.

Before he could come up with a sane-sounding answer, Tatum tapped on the door. "Sheriff, a call just came in. A large man in a mask was spotted wandering around the houses on Patrick Ave."

Rook's eyes shot to Wzorek, who also perked up. He then looked back to Tatum.

Tatum's shirt was half-tucked in and his hair stuck out at the cowlick. He had been in bed when he was called with the news. He looked at Rook and Rook saw pain and confusion. Tatum was in a daze. Shaken to the core, yet unsure how to react to death of a brother he only recently discovered he had, he didn't understand how his friend had gotten wrapped up, how Rook could even be suspect for such gruesome murders, or possibly he couldn't understand how he hadn't seen the murderous sociopath that lurked behind Rook's eyes.

Don't worry, you didn't overlook anything. There's no *murderous sociopath in here . . . normally.* Rook didn't know how to convey the message. He didn't know what

126

to do in general. He had landed smack in the middle of shit creek without a paddle.

"You want me to go check it out?" Tatum asked Wzorek.

"I'm coming with you. Lock Rook up for now. We have to hold him for further questioning."

Without a word, Tatum unhooked him and escorted him to the holding cell next to the one where Benedict had been. Neither man knew what to say. Rook needed a plan and Tatum needed proof, one way or the other.

Duke eyed them from his doggie bed in the corner, muzzle resting on top of his red ball.

His cell was identical to the others. Painted gray bars held him in, a stone slab with a thin mattress on it jutted from the wall, and a foot away a stainless steel toilet lay bathed with germs. He stepped in, turned around, and stuck his hands through the bars to have the cuffs removed.

Tatum silently obliged without looking Rook in the eye again. He clipped the cuffs to his belt and left the room.

Rook grabbed the bars in his hands and pressed his head between them. He was alone. Well, as alone as he could be with Apxutaraxi kicking around.

Duke eyed him for a while longer, rose to his feet, and tentatively sauntered over.

Rook squatted and scratched the underside of his snout.

The dog growled at him and then whimpered and lowered his head to his paws. He was as confused as Tatum. He instinctively knew he was in the presence of evil, and yet felt the kind heart still beating in Rook's chest. He padded back to his bed.

"You too, huh?" The station was empty, so he talked to the dog, not that he would've had qualms anyway. "If you have any ideas, I'm all ears."

He stood and walked to the stone slab and thin mattress. The small, coach-class, airline-quality pillow they had provided was surprisingly comfortable. He put his hands behind his head, in much the same position Benedict had been, and wondered how many other jails offered pillows. It was almost certainly Rose's doing.

The lights in the jail switched off audibly. For a moment he was left in complete darkness, and then, as his eyes adjusted, he realized a soft light was coming from the front of the station where Rose's desk was. Sue and Tatum had locked up and left. Surely he wasn't entirely alone? It couldn't have been standard procedure to leave a detainee unsupervised in a dark cell. Granted, Duke kept a watchful eye.

He strained to see the dog bed in the corner, only to find that Duke was gone. Somehow the dog had managed to slink off without making a sound.

He heard footsteps coming from the hallway where the morgue was attached. They weren't canine. Someone had entered the building through the same entrance the paramedics used, and they were shuffling along.

Crrrrrrrsht.

Plunk.

Crrrrrrrrsht.

Plunk.

Mitchell Henderson came to mind. He had seen the paramedics wheel his remains into the building for Dr. Harper to reassemble. He could see Mitchell, or the rotting carcass that had once been Mitchell, thumping down the hall. Mitchell had become a Frankenstein of parts so twisted you couldn't tell they had all originally been his. Seams in his leg, reattached just below the knee, popped as he dragged the leg along and put weight on it. A yellow pus with pink swirls oozed out of each stitched area in his leg, his thighs, his arms, and through the several dozen stab wounds in his chest and stomach. Organs that had been stuffed back in peeked out through the gashes. He was still missing a hand, and in his other he clutched the two fingers that they had found. His face was a fragmented mess. Dr. Harper had been unable to piece it back together effectively. Half his scalp was missing, and on the other side, one milky eye peered at Rook.

The body had to have been shipped off by then,

and yet Rook could smell the fetid flesh. The air grew increasingly putrid as the noise got louder. He gagged.

Crrrrrrrsht.

Plunk.

From his cell he could see a shadow striding against the wall through the slit of a window in the door. Someone really was coming.

"Hello!? Who's there?!" He couldn't do much.

There was no answer.

Crrrrrrrsht.

Plunk.

He backed up against his bed.

Crrrrrrrsht.

Plunk.

The noise stopped. He waited for the Frankenstein creature to burst through the door, but nothing happened. Minutes passed. The dark jail remained quiet. He stepped forward once more and looked to the door. It was a latch door with a green lock. The walls around it had turned to brick. It was *his* door.

"Deep."

He jumped back and screamed. Jon had appeared at the cell door. His neck was swollen and purple around the slit from the knife. Dried blood streaked down his chest. In his hand was the source of the shuffling, scraping sound. He had been dragging the head of his shiny, highly priced ax against the floor, the same ax Rook used to hack his way out of Jon's house and then buried in the woods a mile away from his property.

Rook looked at him, wide-eyed and speechless.

"Deep!"

Jon wheezed out the word angrily. His face contorted to an expression opposite the smile Rook remembered. It was anguish, it was sorrow, and it was anger.

"Deep! Deep! Deep!"

Jon repeated the last word he had spoken over and over. He flung the ax back over his shoulder and then heaved it forward with all his might. It clanged loudly as it bounced off the panel housing the locking mechanism of the cell door.

"DEEP!"

He swung again. The metal shrieked as the ax wedged in the weld between the bar and the locking panel. Jon bared his teeth and growled like an animal. He freed the ax and changed the angle of his swing. He struck the lock horizontally with another loud clang. The cell door stood triumphant, although Jon didn't seem to register the shock that should have been shooting up his arms as the ax bounced off the metal.

Rook remembered the feeling of an inside fastball hitting the handle of an aluminum bat. His hands stung for the rest of that game. It wasn't time to remember the baseball team his foster parents had forced him onto, though. A dead man wielding a very capable ax was set at getting to him.

With another growl, Jon did the unexpected. He got the door open. Whether due to an old decrepit state or due to the supernatural force being exerted upon it, the lock gave way. With one last swing, the door exploded open and bounced off the bars. Jon stepped in, ax in hand.

Rook backed up into the corner, unsure what to do. He was an unarmed man against an armed, undead creature. He entertained the idea of charging and trying to gain control of the ax for only a moment and then dismissed it.

Jon shuffled closer, dragging the ax once more, panting.

Every muscle in Rook's body tensed in preparation of an explosive attempt to flee, and yet he was frozen.

Jon got within arm's reach and stared Rook in the eyes. He was close enough for his musky, slightly rancid breath with a hint of copper to reach Rook's nostrils. His brow wrinkled over his milky, white eyes.

"Deeeeep."

It sounded as if he was pleading.

"Deeeeeeeeeeeeeeeeeeeeeeeeeep." His voice rasped more out of the hole in his throat than from his mouth.

Rook slid out of the corner with his back to the bars.

Jon only turned his head.

"Deep."

It came out like a mournful sigh.

Rook pushed off the bars and ran past Jon. He grabbed the ax and shut the door behind him. Not that it would hold anyway.

Jon turned, gargling, unable to form the word anymore. His head snapped back violently. Dirty, white fingers wriggled out of his neck and tore his head farther apart. A ghoulish face squeezed out like candy from a Pez dispenser. The face was strikingly pale and smiled wickedly through motor oil saliva.

"Sorry, Jon. I don't think Rookie got the message." The face was Apxutaraxi and, more horrifyingly, it looked like Rook's "father." It was as if his "father" had crawled from his grave and fresh flesh was stretched over his face.

Jon's head fell to the floor as Apxutaraxi tore out and shed him like a snakeskin.

Rook tightened his grip on the ax and kept it ready to strike.

"Now, now, is that any way to greet your father?" Apxutaraxi wagged a slender finger. He was somewhere between tendril creature and "father."

Rook remained poised.

"You think you can stop me?" Apxutaraxi laughed. "Give it up. You've been a tough nut to crack, but I'm almost there. You can either open that door and show me what it is you fear most . . ." He pointed a hand toward the door with the green lock. His arm stretched out more than humanly possible.". . . Or I'll open it myself after I butcher more of your friends."

Seeing his "father" stirred up a strongly rooted anger in Rook. The man was dead, and for good reason. He wanted him to die all over again.

Apxutaraxi cackled ecstatically. "I AM anger!"

"I AM death!"

"I AM fear!"

"The more you create, the stronger I get. So hate me!" he yelled and then grinned.

Rook closed his eyes and concentrated on a happy memory, on Carol and Richard.

A cold hand clamped around his neck and choked him.

"LOOK AT ME!" Apxutaraxi screamed at him.

He looked and was eye to eye with evil.

"You want Carol and Richard? Let's look at Carol and Richard . . ."

Chapter 21

Rose's rocking chair creaked under her as she swayed back and forth. She was in the living room wrapped up in her favorite blanket reading a Danielle Steele novel. She had a cold glass of iced tea next to her, and George was in bed, sleeping a heavy, drug-induced sleep. He had been asleep for hours while she read through the night and into the morning.

She'd fed him meatloaf, a couple hard-boiled eggs, a crisp dill pickle, some au gratin potatoes, and a garden salad on the side before giving him his medication and tucking him in for the night. He didn't like the salad, but she told him he couldn't still have all his favorite foods without integrating more greens. It was a small victory in the day-to-day war she fought with him as she tried to nurse him back to health. She loved the man, though, so she'd fight her hardest until he was back to his old self. In the meantime, she enjoyed her retreats into Steele's worlds.

She put her *Chronicles of Narnia* bookmark, a gift from her nephew, at the end of a chapter and paused for a drink. The tea was sweet with a hint of lemon. The cubes clinked in her glass. She savored the flavor on her lips and stared out the double-wide window overlooking the patio. She stretched and yawned and watched the ice still falling from the sky. The storm wasn't excessively powerful, but it had more longevity than originally forecasted and was supposed to leave an accumulation of almost an inch of ice. Power lines would be down and trees would be snapped by the time the storm was done.

Beyond the falling ice, across the street, alongside the neighbor's house, she saw a man. He was huge.

133

Even in the dark, she could tell he was close to seven feet tall. He wasn't lanky like a basketball player either. He was wide and thick and, disconcertingly, he was wearing a mask.

With her reading light on, he could've very easily seen her, but it didn't seem he had. She thought about turning it off quickly but didn't want to draw attention that way. Instead, she watched.

He didn't move. He stared forward like a sentinel waiting command. Then he turned and looked directly at her. He stepped forward, and his previously shadowed hand revealed the glint of a knife.

Rose didn't hesitate. As soon as she saw the knife, she ran to the coffee table where she had set her cell phone and dialed the station. Normally the sheriff had to be called directly after hours, but given recent events, they'd appointed Deputy Driggs to work a graveyard shift at the station in case there was any further activity. Driggs couldn't do much more than sit behind Rose's desk with his cast anyway.

He answered on the second ring. "Kyruht Police Station."

"Kevin!" She addressed him by his first name. "It's Rose . . ."

"Oh, hey, Rose. Did you hear about what happened at Distance?"

She didn't ask about Distance. "There's a large man in a mask wandering around my neighborhood, Kevin. I think he has a knife. Call Sue immediately and get someone over here."

"A man in a mask? All right, I'll . . ."

She heard someone walk into the station on Deputy Driggs's end and heard him talking.

"Hey, Tatum, go tell Sheriff Wzorek that there's a masked man out at Rose's place on Patrick Ave." Then he added, "She sounds scared."

As soon as she heard him put his mouth back to the receiver, she questioned him. "Sue and Tatum are there? What's going on?"

"There have been two more murders. Two employees

were stocking and cleaning the place and..." He paused. "It's bad, Rose. The sheriff is talking to that Rook guy right now"

Rook? A china plate fell and shattered in the kitchen. Her heart leapt.

"Get someone out here now!"

She hung up the phone.

After what seemed like an eternity of waiting, she approached the kitchen. The backdoor had been locked, but she doubted it would have been much trouble for a man of that size. Cautiously she pushed the swinging door open with her fingertips until it was cracked enough for her to see in. A china plate had fallen from its holder in the shelving near the backdoor. It lay in pieces on the checkered tile floor.

She heard a soft moan issue from upstairs.

George! She ran to the staircase.

The steps were carpeted and were kind enough not to creak under her as she crept upstairs. She clenched a butcher's knife she had grabbed from the kitchen in her hand. At the top of the stairs she passed George's shoe polishing clutter in the corner. As a boy, he had been apprentice to a cobbler and maintained the habit for as long as he was healthy. A floorboard in the hallway squeaked. She froze. After more silence, she continued to the bedroom at the end of the hall.

"George?" she called out in a whisper and minded every step she took.

"George, was that you? Are you all right?"

With no reply, Rose feared the worst and ran into the room without a further thought.

George was on his side facing away from her. His bald spot glistened with perspiration from one of his many night sweats. He didn't stir.

She walked around the foot of the bed. She had to see his face and see that he was breathing to be sure.

The sheets around his chest were stained red. He had been stabbed several times just below the neck. His eyes were closed and it looked like he had slept through the whole thing, though she knew he hadn't.

Hot tears streaked down her cheeks and she resisted the urge to scream. A grief she had never before known crushed her lungs and left her struggling for breath.

The man stepped out from a shadowy corner he'd been waiting in and took her in two swift strides. He held her from behind, needing only one powerful arm, and put his knife to her throat.

She thought of her wedding day with George and how handsome he looked in his tuxedo. She let the butcher knife fall from her side and shut her eyes.

Chapter 22

He remembered almost every detail about that cold, winter night and would remember as long as he lived. November 21st had been the same as any other day nearing the end of that month. The snow hadn't been particularly heavy. A light blanket three or four inches deep covered the land. The temperature, however, had been fierce. Nighttime lows frequently dropped below zero with wind chill, even though it was early winter.

That didn't keep young Rook from sledding during the day. He hadn't made any friends in the six months he'd been with Carol and Richard, so he was by himself atop the snowy hill. Alone and viciously bitten by every gust of wind, he still smiled, rosy-cheeked, as he looked over the white land and dusted treetops. Boots had left a trail behind him, leading back to the ranch. He was still technically in his "parents' backyard," though he applied both terms loosely in his thoughts. Carol and Richard were great—hell, they were amazing—but naming them "parents" would be derogatory in his eyes. A couple dozen acres was also more than a "backyard."

Admiring the smoothed tracks he had sledded into the hillside, as well as their bright sheen in the sunlight, he couldn't help but smile. He was away from *them* and didn't have to worry about any men's size thirty-six belts, black eyes, or dingy backrooms. At the thought of the belts, the scars in his back stung with a burn that even the wind couldn't dispel. *Never again*, he thought to himself. At nine, he was more mature and aged than anyone else in his class. He wished he wasn't.

The dangerous thoughts creeping into his mind couldn't grab a foothold. The day was too perfect. He hadn't a worry in the world. All he had to do all day was sled down the hill on his plastic red agent of gravity and walk back up. When he was ready, he would return home and Carol would have hot cocoa waiting for him. Richard was supposed to be sledding with him, but Richard was too wrapped up in his latest masterpiece. He didn't mind, though. He preferred to be alone. Rook also admired Richard for his honest work and the love he had for it. One day he hoped to be like Richard.

He took one last survey of his view from the top and then plopped down. He counted to three in his head, rocking back and forth, and then pushed. Within seconds, he was whizzing down the hill at breakneck speeds. He tried to keep his eyes open, but the snow kicked up in front of the sled and began its usual assault on his cheeks. He imagined he was sliding down some icy cavern in a gutsy attempt to outrun yetis, from whom he'd stolen a magic snow cone. He could taste the blue raspberry from the cone on his lips.

Three quarters of the way down the hill, he hit a bump he had deliberately aimed for and got about a foot of air that, at first, grew and then rapidly decreased as he proceeded in his descent. Finally, the sled reconnected with a thud that sent Rook rolling off. He tumbled for a while, exaggerated a roll or two, and then came to rest in a drift at the bottom of the hill, laughing into the snow and then grabbing a mouthful. The powdery white snow made stubble on his chin.

Carol wouldn't have liked him deliberately wiping out, but she wasn't around. A particularly potent gust of wind made him realize he actually was freezing. His face felt stiff and hard. Snow that had cached around his ankles found its way into his boots as well. His toes were bordering on that oxymoronic, painfully numb feeling. With a sigh, he trudged back up the hill toward the ranch, wiggling his toes as he walked.

The rusty, red pickup truck in the driveway didn't immediately catch his attention, as he later thought it should have, nor was it the horses whinnying madly in the stable. It was a single black raven resting gingerly atop the snow that captured him. Ravens weren't uncommon. To see the solitary bird, even one of such size at that time of year, wasn't unusual. Ravens did as they pleased, whenever they pleased, but something about this particular bird was odd. It wasn't scratching through the snow for some hidden nugget of frozen carrion or even moving at all. It was watching him with full attention. He took one step closer and it cawed angrily, seemingly telling him to back off. Another step, then two more, and the bird remained fixed on him as he tiptoed by. There was something off about the bird. He wasn't an expert, but it looked different than a regular raven. The closer he got to the house, the more agitated the creature became. Finally, it took off toward him in a fury of squawking and flapping wings.

He would've liked to think that the scratching talons and beating wings were God's way of trying to keep him away that day, but the bird wasn't some secret messenger or protector trying to push him away. The fact was that, no matter the intentions, the bird hastened his steps back to the house. There was no God at the ranch that day.

He burst through the backdoor as fast as he could. It was unlocked, as most country doors were. The back entry led directly into the kitchen. It was in that kitchen that Carol had baked pies for Rook. Whole pies, apple, pumpkin, blueberry, rhubarb, coconut crème, and many others had all been made from scratch with utmost precision and that special ingredient only the most caring cooks seem to know about. Carol happily played housewife and tended to the ranch with Richard while they subsisted primarily on his royalty checks. Rook thought he had finally died and gone to heaven when they brought him home and he smelled that first pumpkin pie bathing the house in an irresistible aroma. It was a smell that made you deliberately inhale bites of the air just to savor the flavor. It was that smell he would remember her by.

Rook glanced at a boiling pot on the stove and thought he smelled mashed potatoes instead of hot chocolate. She must have just stepped away from dinner. There was no direct path to the living room from the kitchen, so he had to either go down the hall or traverse Richard's office to make it to the sacred boob tube. The hallway connected to the kitchen branched off to the bathroom and bedrooms with an opening on the far right that exposed the living room. He tracked several steps of snow in before he realized it and stopped to pry off his boots and peel away his snow pants. After a quick one-foot dance to get the snow pants off, he proceeded to the office. It was the longer route, but he liked to see Richard at work.

Richard was a good man. He was the kind of "father" who would make time to toss the football around with Rook or take him out for ice cream, but when he was in the zone, there was no waking him. He would be gone for hours on end and never really come out of the daze for weeks at a time when he was writing his thrillers. Benjamin Kreager's adventures as a detective provided Rook with the cushy life he happily embraced, and even when he was zoned out, Richard was still better than Rook's actual "father" by light years.

Once he had spilled juice while running through the office. He instantly froze and cringed, waiting for the inevitable cursing and thrashing, but Richard never raised his voice. Instead, he calmly cleaned up the juice and scooped Rook up in his lanky arms. Rook was small for his age at the time. Still, most people wouldn't have been able to scoop him up like Richard did. He sat Rook on his computer chair, tussled his hair, and said, "Don't worry about it, bud. Wanna see what I've been working on?" They both stared at the Packard Bell screen, its soft glow welcoming. Richard undoubtedly was working out plot points as he stared over Rook's shoulder and through the screen. Rook was too shocked to make sense of the words in front of him. He hadn't been beaten. No, Richard was instead sharing a whole world with him.

When he entered the office, Richard's computer screen was lit and a taunting cursor was waiting to begin a new paragraph. There was no soft clicking of keys on the computer's keyboard, though. The office was quiet. The living room, however, was not. Rook could hear arguing, a woman pleading, Richard defiantly saying "No," and a third voice that made his insides tighten as if his body was trying to curl into itself.

"Give me the boy now!"

It was Jackie Spencer, his biological "father." All at once, the walls around Rook collapsed away, his heart stopped beating, and his head started spinning. It was all a dream. Jackie was coming to collect him and take him back to Hell.

"Please Jackie! P-p-p-lease! Don't hurt anyone. I just want my baby back!"

Rook also recognized the pleading voice before he peeked around the corner and saw them. His "mother" was pleading with Jackie just to grab Rook and run. Jackie, on the other hand, seemed to have more in mind. He was waving a gun around. Rook couldn't tell what kind, but it was silver with a brown handle and looked big enough to make quick work of them all.

Richard was standing between them and Carol with his arms wide beside him: a protective stance. He was taller and skinnier than Jackie and his blonde hair was well kept, unlike Jackie's mane of scraggily black hair, but Jackie wasn't a slouch. He was a thick six feet and Rook knew what he was capable of.

Carol was frozen behind Richard, the phone clutched firmly in her hand. It was impossible to tell if she'd already dialed the police or had been stopped before she was able. Carol may have played housewife, but she didn't look it. She more closely resembled Barbie with her long, blond hair, overachieving bust, and slender waist. Most people thought she was a wife Richard bought with his money, but they had known each other before he had his first best seller. He was just a lucky man, usually.

His luck didn't look like it was going to hold out much longer. Jackie was more jacked up and out of control than Rook had ever seen him, which was saying a lot. Judging from the thick bristle on his chin and jaw, he hadn't bothered to shave for a while. His lips were chapped and cracked with blood. His missing incisor, a memento from his boxing days, no longer had a gold tooth holding residence. He'd probably sold it to score meth or heroine, whatever he was injecting those days. His greasy mess of hair was as disconcerting as ever.

The first time Rook was led through the door into the dingy backroom, he looked back at his "father" only to see he'd already turned away. The last thing he had seen before his innocence was completely torn away was the back of his "father's" head as he walked away. He *walked away*, counting cash in his hand as he walked. More troubling still were his eyes. Rook thought he saw the devil in those eyes. There was no humanity in them.

"I'm gonna give you one last chance. Give me the fucking boy." Jackie wanted his moneymaker back. Plus, it would shut the bitch up.

Rook's "mother" Lynn was on her knees, weeping at Jackie's side. She still had long, auburn hair, but her face was gaunt and shriveled under an overapplication of gaudy makeup. The skin was tight on her cheekbones and the meat of her actual cheeks all but vanished into hollows on either side of her mouth. Her habits had made her look thirty years older than she was. He didn't need to see them to know that bruise-surrounded holes riddled the inside of her arms. Apparently her drug of choice hadn't changed. Rook remembered the empty kisses she had given him. Her hot breath reeked of smoke. He also remembered how she trembled when she held him. Whether it was fear or junkie shakes between fixes was irrelevant. She meant nothing to him. She had turned away from him, too, in her own way. Just do what Jackie says, Rook. Then maybe you'll only bleed for a day.

Richard had hunting rifles locked up in the cellar. Rook knew where the key was hidden. He had found it when he was looking for the dark secrets he was sure Richard and Carol had to have. Taped under the dresser had been Jackie's favorite spot to hide the baggies he didn't want Lynn to find. He could run to the bedroom, grab the key from where it was taped under the dresser, and then take the kitchen stairs next to the pantry down to the cellar without being noticed. They hadn't seen him spying around the corner of the office. He could make it. Richard and Carol just had to hang on. Before he left, he heard Richard stalling while he worked out a plan.

"Why do you want him? You never wanted him before."

Au contraire, Richard, au contraire, thought Rook. They didn't want him at first, but once Jackie figured out how to make money, he was a hot commodity. That, and through the drug-induced haze, Lynn still retained some sort of bizarre motherly desire.

"For shits and giggles. . . . HE BELONGS TO ME!!!" Jackie exploded and smashed a vase that had been minding its own business on a table near the entryway. It exploded into a hundred pieces, some of which cut his hand.

Lynn continued sobbing her confused desires. "P-please. Just give me my baby. T-then he won't hurt no one."

"Shut your mouth, cunt," Jackie hissed at her.

Rook wasted no time. He spun around and sprinted through the office as swiftly as he could. His damp socks made no noise on the carpet. As he shot out of the office and rounded the corner from the kitchen to the hallway, he slipped on the checkered tile. A searing flash of pain shot through his head as it bounced off the floor. Stars shot across his vision, yet he clambered back to his feet. There was no time to nurse the knot that was developing on the back of his head. He prayed they hadn't heard his skull jostling.

The word "contraire" wouldn't leave his mind as he ran down the hall, past the pictures Carol had insisted taking of the three of them in cowboy outfits, a space background, and winter sweaters—separately, of course. A space cowboy wearing a red and green sweater with white trees on it was absurd. He had learned "contraire" from Richard as part of his word-a-day game. He liked that game. He wanted to learn more words from Richard and take more cheesy pictures for Carol. He needed to hurry, for them. They didn't deserve this. It was his nightmare, not theirs.

A pang of guilt surged him forward. The second door on the left was graciously located before the entrance to the living room. They would have surely seen him had he needed to run across. He burst into the master bedroom and frantically searched his hand under the white mahogany dresser. The key wasn't there. A piece of torn scotch tape hung where it had been. The police would later tell him that Richard had the key on him. It looked like he had seen the rusty, red beater pulling up the driveway and got as far as retrieving the key before Jackie kicked in the door.

Rook would break the glass on the gun case. He had no choice. He sprinted out of the bedroom and to the basement steps. The pot on the stove was boiling over and the smell of something burning had replaced that of the mashed potatoes. He was halfway down the steps and could feel the temperature changing when he heard the shots. Any basement is cooler than the rest of the house, especially in the winter, and he could feel the drop with every step. As the cold air encircled him and the first shot rang, he heard Carol scream. A quick second and third shot were followed by silence.

Carol and Richard were gone. Rook was alone in the house with *them*. His legs buckled beneath him and he crumpled into a ball on the steps. He grabbed his knees and closed his eyes as tight as he could. He didn't breathe. He was afraid that if he did, sobs would escape. They did anyway. Warm tears streaked down his face.

It was only when he heard footsteps in the kitchen behind him that he moved. Carol and Richard deserved more mourning than he could ever give them, but sitting on the steps, waiting for Jackie to find him wouldn't honor them. He had to hide and, if necessary, fight.

***

Jackie knew the kid had to be in the house. He had heard a thud in the kitchen when the tall blond was stalling. He wasn't stalling anymore, was he? Jackie laughed to himself. The bitch was still in the living room crying over spilt blood. She wanted the kid, didn't she? Those two weren't going to hand him over free and clear, no hassle. *Hey Jackie, take the boy and we'll throw in twenty pounds of meat from our deep freeze and a case of Bud Light!*

144

He walked through the writer's office first, but there weren't any hiding spots in there for the brat. In the kitchen he spotted dinner on the stove. *Aww, home-cooked meals for Rookie.* He ran his hand across the countertop. Every knife was in its exact spot in the wooden holder. A quintuplet group of bananas was nestled in a hammock, someone's clever pun. There were matching porcelain lighthouse salt and pepper shakers, undoubtedly souvenirs, and a spice rack with carefully labeled bottles of fresh spices was securely mounted above the oven. The kid had it good with Mr. and Mrs. Perfect.

He peered into the pot boiling over, moved it off the burner, and turned off the stove. He couldn't have the place going up in flames before he got the kid. There were boots, mittens, and snow pants in a puddle of melted snow near the door. Rook was definitely inside.

"Come out, come out, wherever you are!" Jackie taunted.

The door next to the pantry was ajar. The kid had run downstairs.

Flicking on the light and taking each step down carefully, he continued, "I know you're down here, Rookie. Stop hiding from your father!"

The gun was still in Jackie's hand, which was dripping blood from the entryway vase's retaliation. He wasn't going to shoot the kid, but he could scare the shit out of him with it, or maybe even burn him with the muzzle since it was still hot from dispatching the two upstairs. *Would you like that, Rook? It would be just like one of your cigarette burns.*

The basement was fairly large but only half-finished. The far wall and accompanying corners remained hidden in shadow. The kid could've been hiding anywhere on that side. For a guy as loaded as blondie, the place wasn't much. He kept it simple and the basement seemed to be entirely storage. There were boxes of decorations, old clothes, books, an unused weight bench, and a gun cabinet. The gun cabinet caught his eye. The glass was broken out.

"Are you going to shoot me, Rookie?" He laughed. "I

bet you can't even hold a rifle straight. Hell, you can't even get your dick straight yet boy."

He felt the end of the rifle at the base of his skull immediately after he'd spoken.

***

Rook had been hiding under the stairs with the first gun he could grab. It was Richard's Browning A-Bolt II and he had fired it before. Richard had taught him at the end of summer. They shot old coffee cans and wine bottles off a fence post at the far end of the property.

There was a moment of silence and then, "Pull the trigger, boy." Jackie urged him on. "PULL THE FUCKING TRIGGER!"

Click. The hollow sound of an empty chamber reverberated across the room and into the darkness. He reflexively tried to fire again, but Jackie turned around, grabbed the rifle, and smashed him with the butt of the handgun above his left eye. A gash immediately opened and started pouring blood. The impact made his brain feel like it pancaked against the back of his skull.

Rook fell limp and lifeless to the floor.

"Damn it, kid, look what you made me do."

Leaving the ranch was a blur. Slumped over Jackie's shoulder and fading in and out of consciousness, Rook awoke long enough to see the trail of blood he was dripping behind. It was brighter when he splattered on the kitchen tile than when they walked through the office and the carpet absorbed it. Then it became a muddy, maroon color.

In the living room Rook's "mother" was still on her knees, tears glistening on her cheeks as she looked at Carol's awkwardly angled body. Carol had taken two shots to the chest and stomach before twisting over the top of the couch and falling to rest arched over. The phone was still in her hand.

Richard had taken a single slug to the head and plastered the wall with bone fragments, bits of brain, and Detective Benjamin Kreager. Skin and hair still covered a portion of the missing matter, giving his head the look of a half-deflated basketball. The force had spun him, as well. He was slumped at the back of the couch near Carol's legs, facing Rook. His eyes were open, but empty. No soul danced behind them. No life pulsed.

Rook blacked out again.

In the distance he could hear Lynn in disbelief. "You killed them! You KILLED them!"

Jackie growled at her, "You're gonna join them if you don't shut your cocksucker!"

She got quiet.

He saw giant, black snakes writhing and hissing in his haze. He didn't know how he could see them, but coiled up in tree roots, they looked like tires washed down by some raging river to his left. Drums beat fervently in his ears. He faced the river. The water was high and violent. White caps surged and carried entire uprooted trees downstream. The raven screamed.

Rook was lying in the bench seat of the truck. Lynn was screaming outside. She was terrified, but angry at Jackie. Those nice people didn't need to die. Jackie hit her, and then again. She fell to her knees. The snow soaked the knees of her jeans; the gravel underneath cut at her. She stayed quiet.

He was looking up at Lynn in the truck. He had no idea how much time had passed or how far they were from the ranch. His head rested in her lap, swaying back and forth, and the truck chugged along. She dabbed at the gash above his eye as upside-down evergreens whizzed by the window. His head throbbed, but what hurt worse was the guilt clamped around his chest, choking away every breath. Carol's zucchini bread came to mind, and sweaters, those damn Christmas sweaters. Fresh tears streamed down his face.

Jackie negotiated behind the steering wheel with ease. Four-wheel drive was barely even needed on the plowed road on which he was making his getaway. The corners were a little slick, but nothing he couldn't handle with one bloody hand on the wheel.

The gun in Jackie's waistband gave a brief glint as

the headlights of an oncoming car went by. His face was cold and expressionless. The brutal murders didn't show in him at all. There was nothing, not a single emotion, on which their deaths could've made any impression. The only thing Rook had ever seen from him was rage.

Lynn began to cry again, as well. Jackie's hardest punch couldn't knock her quiet forever.

"I got your precious baby back. Is that not good enough for you, bitch? Am I not good enough for you? Hmm?" He was about two rhetorical questions away from smacking her again.

Then Lynn did something none of them ever expected. With her swollen eye, scratched cheek, and tear-smudged mascara running all the way down to her lips, she looked into Rook's eyes, kissed his forehead, reached over him without unlocking her eyes, grabbed at Jackie's crotch, and pulled the trigger.

Over Jackie's wild, dickless screaming and the screeching of tires, Rook and Lynn shared one moment. In that moment she said more to him with her eyes than she had ever said in any manner his whole life. It was her fault. She should've stopped the monster long ago and kept Rook from horrible things. She wouldn't turn away anymore. She hoped he could, in some small part, forgive her. The gun was to be her final act, her only real act at all. She was sorry.

Jackie lost control. The truck careened to the left, hit mountainside, and flipped. The world floated around them for one peaceful moment in the chaos. Then the truck landed on its top, the frame collapsed around them, and Rook fell against Lynn on the ceiling. Three more rolls continued them toward the embankment on a curve they had been approaching. The rotted tin can caved in further with each bump. A dilapidated coffin of rusted metal was closing in around them. The coffin hit the guardrail and flipped one last time, sending them over the edge. Once again, on the roof, or what was left of it, gravity clawed them downward. The truck was nothing more than a toy being swatted around until it finally came to rest against trees through which even gravity couldn't pull it.

When Rook once more regained consciousness, his head was spinning. One too many hits on the noggin had finally knocked something loose. The truck wouldn't stop rotating. Things kept getting near, then far, then near again. He turned to get his hands and knees toward the ground, or what he assumed was the ground, and saw what had cushioned him against the brunt of the blows: Lynn. She was broken and lifeless, eyes closed. He looked at her shrunken, wrinkled face and things began to focus. Jackie wasn't in the truck with them. Rook hoped he had been thrown from the vehicle and snapped in two against a tree somewhere.

He crawled out of the smashed window frame, bits of glass cutting his palms. The gash on his forehead was soaking his shirt in blood once more. In the distance, he heard sirens. It was too quick to be an accident response. Carol did dial 911 before she was killed.

He had to get back to the top of the hill or they would never find him, not unless there was enough of the truck left on the road to alert them to the crash. He couldn't take that chance. When he tried to stand, his ankle exploded in pain. It was broken. He could feel a hundred other bumps, cuts, and scrapes. There was one particularly nasty gash below his elbow, but his head and his ankle blew everything else away.

Rook fell to his knees again.

"Help me!" he shouted. "Somebody, please, help me!" He grew louder still.

His tattered body had managed to crawl halfway up the slope, hands and knees frozen by the snow, when he heard the sirens stop above him. He collapsed. They were going to rescue him.

Something grabbed him by the ankle and the pain exploded up his leg again. It was Jackie. He screamed, more from fear than the pain. Jackie was crawling, too. His tibia and fibula had been shattered in his right leg, which he dragged limp behind him, along with the original pelvic injury the bullet had caused. He was half a man. One of his eyes was swollen shut. It was hard to tell if the eye was even there or if it had ruptured in the blunt trauma that mangled his face. His other eye, however, burned with rage.

"You little fucker!" Jackie growled at Rook through broken teeth and gargled blood.

Rook could feel his heart in his throat. The beat was painfully strong and irregular. His peripheral vision faded first, leaving him staring down a dark tunnel at Jackie's damaged body.

Jackie pulled up and propped himself on his left arm. Any weight placed below the waist had to be excruciating. Still, he held himself on arm and midsection. The other arm he raised above his head, brass knuckles begging to bash Rook's head in. He always had those knuckles on him. One of his favorite pastimes was beating money out of "Fish," what he called the cold, slippery sons-of-bitches who tried to squirm out of a payment on one of his bets. In all the turmoil his prized knuckles had never left his pocket, until then.

The all-too-familiar darkness of a blackout cradled Rook again. In the distance he heard a gunshot pound through the trees and a man telling Jackie to lower his fist. *Bad word choice*, he thought. He felt Jackie swing forward and then a second shot blasted, tearing through Jackie's neck and severing his jugular. He bled out almost instantly, leaving Rook unconscious and bathed in blood.

Chapter 23

Rook shot upright on the jail bed. He choked and gasped for breath as if he had just breached the surface of a lake. Beads of sweat plastered his hair against his forehead. His white-knuckled hands gripped the sides of the thin mattress. His stomach wrenched and he lurched toward the toilet. Gripping the sides with disregard for the filth, he vomited up a bitter, watered-down bile. He vomited until only dry heaves remained and then collapsed back into the bed.

It took several minutes of recuperation before he could focus enough to examine his surroundings. He was still in the cell, alone, but the lights were on and the door was open.

The door didn't look beaten with an ax, as it had been in his dream. Rather, it looked as if someone had come along with the key. Beyond the door the soft drywall was dented inward as if he had burst out of his cell. Something was wrong. He knew he was no longer dreaming or hallucinating, yet it felt as if his demons were out walking around. He knew that all hell had broken loose.

He glanced at the door leading to the morgue hall—everything was normal—and then he looked to the hallway leading up front. Evil radiated from the shadows like heat waves off a hot car in the summer. A blood-smeared crutch rested on the floor and a red trail beckoned him to follow to the front.

Follow he did.

On Rose's desk sat a silver ring replete with keys. It had been carefully replaced after use. At the bottom of the desk was a leg, cast in plaster and braced with metal and screws. It was attached to Deputy Driggs's bullet-riddled body.

In a flash Apxutaraxi shared the murder with him. He tricked the deputy into opening the cell door, at which point Apxutaraxi rushed him, knocking the crutch away, and pinned him against the wall. Apxutaraxi drew Deputy Driggs's weapon and shot him point blank in the chest while holding him by the neck. He smiled a contented smile that had once belonged to Rook while he did it. Driggs wasn't dead, though. Apxutaraxi allowed him to crawl down the hall toward the desk phone. He taunted him, played with him, and before he could reach the phone, Apxutaraxi finished him.

I've been a busy boy with a big surprise to show you . . .

***

Tatum supported Rose's head in his hands. She was dead. The limp neck and gaping wound made that abundantly clear. "Rose . . ." He swallowed hard. "We'll get the bastard."

Sue had gone back to the cruiser to call Berryville for reinforcements. The killer, it seemed, was powerful, quick, and, worst of all, indiscriminate. She would need more men to patrol, to investigate, to protect, and to stop the murders. While they had tiptoed into the house, peeking around corners and minding shadows with guns drawn, the killer had moved right along and disappeared into the night.

Tatum set Rose's head down softly on the wooden floor. He probably shouldn't have touched her at all, but he had instinctively tried to hold her up when they found her on the floor. Her irresistible smile was gone. Her eyes were closed.

He surveyed the room for clues. George was in bed, there was an unused butcher's knife on the floor with Rose, and there were boot prints leading away from the blood. He and Sue had been careful not to contaminate the area with their own prints, and he knew neither of them was wearing a size seventeen boot.

He heard gunshots outside.

Faster than he had ever moved before, Tatum ran

from the room and bounded down the stairs. From the front door he saw Sue in stance with her gun pointed at the masked man who was only ten feet away.

She shouted, "I'm not giving you anymore warning shots! Drop your weapon, put your hands behind your back, and get down on the ground!"

Tatum could see she was hesitant to kill another man, but he knew she could do it. He drew his weapon and pointed it at the man as well.

The man didn't respond in any way. His massive hand remained wrapped tightly around the hunting knife. His legs remained still. He only turned his head to look at Tatum and then looked back to Sue. It was then, in the span of a few horrifying seconds, that he forced them to act.

The masked man exploded into a charge toward Sue. They both fired their weapons. Tatum's shot missed. Sue's landed square in the man's stomach. He was unfazed.

With mind-boggling speed for a man bigger than a fridge, the beast closed the ten feet and slammed into Sue like a train.

Sue instinctively braced herself and Tatum fired a second shot.

Tatum's second shot punched through the man's shoulder, but didn't keep him from impaling Sue with his knife.

She screamed in pain and the knife screamed against the metal body of the car as it ripped through her tiny waist.

Tatum fired one more wild shot in a blind rage of his own and ran at the man. Mike, Rose, Sue, he was running out of friends fast.

In one deft maneuver the man pulled out the knife and heaved it at Tatum. He kept Sue pinned by the throat with his other hand while she fought.

Tatum almost dodged the knife. He turned and ducked simultaneously, but wasn't fast enough to avoid the blade slicing through his left trapezes muscle as it sailed by. He tumbled to the ground and saw Sue give her last effort.

She kicked and swung her fist as hard as she could. When it connected against the man's jaw, she felt two of her fingers break. She wanted to scream in pain once more. The masked man absorbed the blow with nothing more than a tilt of the head. She had trained hard for years and was capable of disarming and incapacitating some of the biggest men, but what was before her was no man. She looked over at Tatum scrambling to his feet and her windpipe was crushed.

Tatum screamed and the monster dropped Sue's lifeless body. Tatum charged one last time and was knocked into oblivion by a brutal haymaker.

Chapter 24

"What have you done?"

I got the ball rolling real good.

Rook stepped out of the police station and into the parking lot. Idling near the entrance with its front wheels over the curb and the driver's door open wide was one of the three cruisers the Kyruht police department owned. The other two were with Wzorek and Tatum, and at the shop for repairs, respectively.

A single light at the far end of the lot flickered. It was a large lot meant to support small crowds when the adjoining community center was used. Rook expected it to be quiet at three in the morning, but it was as if the earth had stopped spinning. Only the engine made a sound as it puttered anxiously.

Hop in.

Apxutaraxi was in control. Rook's limbs obeyed another master.

His legs took him to the door and sat him inside. His hands shut the door and clamped on the steering wheel. His foot poised itself over the pedal. He heard a whimper in the backseat. He fought to move his eyes to the rearview. Apxutaraxi allowed him to see.

Dawn was hog-tied tightly and yelled a muffled scream from behind her gag when she saw Rook. She turned her head away from his gaze and sobbed.

Anger and grief surged through Rook. His hands tightened on the wheel, of his own volition. Apxutaraxi quickly sapped the anger and used it to strengthen his hold on Rook.

Consider her a gift. I'm gonna get you to loosen up kid. And hey . . . we'll loosen her up.

155

Dawn cried louder.

Rook realized Apxutaraxi was audibly speaking through him now. It appeared to Dawn that he was talking to himself. She had been kidnapped and bound by a lunatic.

Apxutaraxi threw the car into gear and floored it in reverse. Apparently he had been a quick study reading through Rook's mind.

We're gonna go pick up a friend.

Apxutaraxi wasn't fooling around anymore. He had finished playing with Rook after the show-and-tell with Driggs. He was commanding and controlling.

Dawn screamed again and rocked her body wildly in a futile attempt.

The car hopped out onto the central highway and went west toward Patrick Avenue. He was going to pick up the black-masked behemoth.

Very good, Rookie. It's time to join my brothers.

Rook strained to see Dawn again and caught a glimpse of himself in the mirror. The black veins had crept up over his shoulder and reached up through his neck. They were visible above his collar. He then realized that the Rook he was looking at still had his eyes forward. He seemed to be drifting while Apxutaraxi just kept gaining more control. The foreign Rook shifted his eyes and locked in on him in the rearview.

He addressed Apxutaraxi. "Why Dawn? How?"

Why? Just look at her! Apxutaraxi was excited. *She's perfect for us.*

It didn't seem like Apxutaraxi was referring to himself and Rook anymore. He was referring to his brothers.

While you were spending quality time with your father, I took a stroll down the street to visit her. EVERYONE is just down the street in this place. We need to move on to the big time, kid. There's a whole big world out there for us to see!

"Won't Wzorek and Tatum being waiting for us there?"

156

Self-preservation. That's what I like about you. Forget the devil inside. Forget the girl tied up in the backseat. Don't let the police lock me away! You're all flight and no fight, Rookie. You always have been. You can't run away from me. You can't hide. And you've proven you certainly can't fight. Don't worry about Wzorek and Tatum. They've been taken care of.

He pulled off on the street before Patrick Avenue. Between the houses in the distance, cherries on the top of the Tatum's cruiser danced. It was hard to tell in the dark, but it looked as if a crowd had been drawn out into the night and was surrounding something, or someone, near the cruiser.

Rook feared the worst, and for good reason. He could feel what Apxutaraxi knew. Wzorek and Tatum had been dealt with in a lethal manner.

What little light there was glistened on the sheen of ice coating the streets and posts. The ice had stopped falling temporarily, but even with the main event yet to come, the vehicle already struggled to come to a stop. The cruiser hopped the curb and came to rest with the front wheels off-road once more.

Apxutaraxi reached over the passenger's side and unlocked the door. Standing beyond was the large man in his black mask. He slipped into the passenger seat swiftly and robotic. The car sagged and then settled as its shock absorbers absorbed the man's weight.

Dawn screamed and cried in the backseat.

Rook was terrified but couldn't move. Apxutaraxi held firm.

The mask hugged tightly against the man's swollen face. His veins bulged grotesquely in his neck. Rook swore he saw one move. It could have been sliding around the muscles in the man's neck. They were grossly oversized as well. The whole man had become a gargantuan monstrosity.

Beautiful, isn't he? My brothers at their best.

Rook wondered if he was doomed to a similar fate.

The man breathed heavily under his mask but remained statuesque, facing forward.

Don't worry. We have something else planned. Even under our influence, you meat sacks only last so long.

Rook could see several wounds on the man and a smattering of mixed blood, both new and old. A dark sludge oozed out of two fresh bullet wounds. He didn't clutch the wounds or hunch over in pain. It seemed he felt nothing.

"Where are we going?" Rook did all he could do: ask questions.

Apxutaraxi didn't respond. Instead, Rook felt a second of worry split through Apxutaraxi's armor of confidence. Minutes passed before Apxutaraxi mumbled.

Vast and empty... azure majestic... lifeless abyss...

He pondered Apxutaraxi's words for several more minutes.

Dawn rustled around in the seat behind them. She may have been up to something. Apxutaraxi and the beast didn't notice or didn't care.

Giving up, he asked another question." Why did you go back to the station and let me wake up there? Why not just keep going?"

You know I like a good game, Rookie.

He knew Apxutaraxi was hiding something. Apxutaraxi had gone back to the station for a reason. He just hadn't the slightest what that reason could be.

Don't strain too hard, kid. Apxutaraxi laughed again. *Time for some new wheels.*

The cruiser pulled off the road into a wooded area, the same wooded area where Rook had hidden his pickup.

Without recollection of the passing seconds, Rook was suddenly outside the driver's door. Apxutaraxi was fazing him out so efficiently now that he was losing whole segments of time.

The large man all but ripped the door off its hinges when he tore Dawn out of the vehicle. She screamed and writhed violently, but to no avail. With one hand on her ropes, he carried her to the truck like a human purse. At least she was still a living human purse and not skinned. She wouldn't be for long, though, if he didn't figure something out.

Time blipped again and Rook was in the driver's seat. Dawn was slumped unconscious on the bench seat between him and the large man. Judging from the fresh-looking knot on her head, she hadn't settled down voluntarily. Her chest rose and fell softly. It was the only indication she was still alive.

Hopefully she wakes up once we get there, eh? It won't be as fun without her kicking and screaming as we hold her down.

"I won't let you."

Apxutaraxi drove without a sense of urgency. He leisurely weaved through the forest, navigating the truck to its destination with the assured confidence of a man going to a knife fight with a bazooka.

Outside the truck ice-laden trees bowed downward. There was a solid quarter-inch of ice coating everything. Ice battled to form on the cold spots of the truck's hood and the window defrosters churned out heat as fast as they could. A quick glance in the rearview revealed a small ice rink in the bed of the truck.

Morning light was beginning to creep through the night and illuminated the sky just enough for his eye to catch something along the treetops. Something large and black was skimming swiftly over the forest, keeping pace behind them. The sky was a dark, bluish gray, but he could tell there was definitely a mysterious creature following them like a shadow. He tried to focus on the shadowy blur and found that there was not one but three. The three figures flew mostly in unison, only occasionally breaking apart as they danced through the trees.

What more could possibly be involved? His nightmare already had spun out of control. Puzzle pieces were piling up and none of them fit. He needed to find a corner piece.

"Deep." Jon's word reverberated through his mind.

He was overlooking something simple. Jon had given him the proverbial puzzle box to look at for instruction, but what was the image? All the madness was rooted in one place: the artifacts, the evil, the brothers, Chief Klamath, the mother. In his rage the chief had blamed their mother and cast her out. She was the key. Jon had said she was tied to a boulder and thrown into the great mountain lake.

The lake.

The deep.

He felt foolish for having missed something so obvious. That's why the Crater Lake brochure almost leveled him when he saw it. Crater Lake hadn't always been named so. It had once been Lake Majesty.

Apxutaraxi's words made more sense.

Someone is figuring it out! Apxutaraxi taunted.

Before that the lake was Blue Lake, named by the settlers, and prior to that, when the natives held the land, it was directly translated as Deep Blue Lake.

All at once, Rook knew what he had to do to end the nightmare. The lake was a symbol of death and of life. An innocent woman had been drowned there, and an evil was born. Life and death, death and life, the lake was a gateway.

*And even though it's a dangerous place for all of us, we're gonna go to the Deep Blue Lake. We have a gift to give our father. . . .*He looked down at Dawn.

Her head swayed as the truck slid briefly on a turn in the road. Outside the ice had changed to snow. They were reaching a higher elevation and the roads, layered in ice and powdered with snow, were increasingly treacherous.

Rook couldn't help but think of his truck ride with Jackie and Lynn. He considered trying to take control of one arm. One arm would be enough to pull the steering wheel and wreck them. He couldn't risk Dawn, though. She was innocent in it all.

She's not as innocent as you want to believe, Rookie. She's not really interested in you. She was curious after I made you man up and kiss her, but she recognized you're just too nice and ran to someone who could really thrill her. Do you want to see what she was doing before I paid her a visit? Or should I say whom? He cackled in delight.

"It doesn't matter. She's innocent in this!" he pleaded, knowing it wouldn't do any good. Apxutaraxi needed her for what he was planning. She wasn't a toy. She was a tool.

What's the matter? Do you fear the loss of innocence?

Rook could hear banging on a metal door. Almost rhythmic, yet wholly savage, it echoed with a percussive force like his head had been strapped to a bass drum. The pounding grew louder and louder, sending tremors through his body. Then, suddenly, silence.

He could see the door. It was his door. The red brick that framed it disappeared into nothingness like it always had. The door itself was dented and broken, however. His green lock was on the ground, still clinging to the latch that had been ripped off. The welds and lock were merely symbols of the depths to which he had gone to hide and isolate the memory. They were mental blocks on a memory. The mental blocks had been removed and the door was opened.

Fully immersed in his own mind, Rook had no sense of the outside world. Apxutaraxi had become dangerously efficient at multi-tasking.

The damaged, gray, steel door hung open on one remaining hinge. The room beyond was dark, except for one overhead light dangling and casting its dim gleam over a heavy, wooden bookstand. On that bookstand sat a terribly large book recounting every detail and every second of every encounter with the fat man. It, too, was open. Rook didn't need to see which equally terrible page it had been left at to discern that Apxutaraxi had gleaned what he needed from it.

The musky, sour scent of fermenting sweat mingled in the air with mild pine and boiled eggs. A bed creaked in the darkness. Rook choked back bitter vomit rising in his throat. His stomach was tightening into a dense ball, filling his esophagus with acid and bile. The boiled eggs and sweat were nauseating enough, let alone with the poorly applied pine-based air freshener on top, but it was the fat man himself who made Rook want to turn inside out.

The box spring of the bed moaned from the

darkness again. "Hey, kiddo. Come over here and say hi."

The voice was nasally but made light to bait in and assure unsuspecting children. Under the soft speaking was labored breath and sluggish pronunciation, both hampered by the pressure of obesity. Fat deposits smothered the sinuses and fat lips sloshed the words around.

The light overhead started to swing slowly off Rook toward the bed as if a hand had been placed directly and deliberately on it. The corroded bronze leg of an old bed frame came into view first.

Rook turned to run, afraid to see what the light had been set upon. He saw Jackie walk away, counting his money as the door swung shut behind him with a loud bang. The room suddenly burst aglow with dirty amber light. Waning sunlight was pouring through smoke-yellowed curtains behind the bed. They were ratty and torn, just like the mattress of the bed. Rook didn't have to look. He had seen the room enough before. He refused to look again.

"Aw. Don't be like that now. Be a sport."

His arms were forced down flat against his sides; his legs turned him around against his will. It was unlike Apxutaraxi's control. It was an external force acting against his body this time, as external as it could be inside his own mind.

His legs looked smaller as they betrayed him. He realized he was a child again. As he turned, he could see the fat man was twisting his fingers to control him like a marionette. With a back and forwards movement between the pointer and middle finger, his legs walked him over to the edge of the bed.

The bed was without sheets and had a gold and white floral design straight out of the seventies. It sagged in several feet in the center over the broken box spring. Along the sides brown metal springs poked out in a half-dozen places like spires of Hell's castle. The floral mattress was stained black in several spots where the fat man didn't completely cover it. The black marks were faded, dried out, washed-out bloodstains.

The fat man was nude. His thighs and overhanging belly kept his genitals covered for the time being. He was pale white and hairy. His calves looked bloated and diseased in their purple hue. The plethora of wiry hairs on his chest and shoulders rose and fell with each breath. He was nearly bald on the top with only a ring of hair around the sides on his head. His nose was bulbous and red like a drinker's. His belly jiggled moderately as his arm and hand directed Rook.

Rook's breathing, which had become erratic, stopped altogether.

"C'mon, little man. Come sit up here with me. I got something I want to show you."

Rook's stomach had rolled up into his throat and was trying to climb out.

"I don't want to." His child voice squeaked out.

"I'm not going to hurt you. Not unless you're bad and disobey your elder." The fat man stared at him. His eyes bulged out of their sockets, more fat deposits at work. "Are you a bad boy, Rookie? Do you want me to hurt you?"

"No," he pleaded. "No, please don't touch me. Don't make me touch you." Hot tears poured down his cheeks.

The fat man grew angry. "Stop crying and get up here!" He forced Rook's hands on to the bed so he could climb up.

"No!" Rook shouted through his tears. He managed to tear his hands away and turn before the fat man tripped him up with his invisible wires of control. He fell on his hands and knees and then into the fetal position. He curled up as tightly as he could, holding his legs so intensely that his hands turned white. He squeezed his eyes shut and tried to imagine a safe place, somewhere he could hide forever and be free of the fat man and Jackie. He thought of the library. The one that had inspired his mind's library.

On rainy days his friends in the neighborhood never wanted to play outside. They would go to their homes, with their parents, and play games and watch movies. He didn't have a home like that to go to. He had Jackie and Lynn. He would instead stay out in the rain and walk anywhere else. It became a hobby of his to go down to the creek during rainstorms and watch the rising waters rush by. The waters flowed fast and to far away places, or so he imagined.

One particular rainy day he found his way to the public library. It was a big, imposing building with oddly Gothic architecture. There were three large arches and long windows and even a couple small steeples. It wasn't true Gothic, but a young architect's recreation. The building briefly served a zealous church, and quite fittingly, was turned into a library after the ministry moved on. He had seen it at a distance before, but never set foot inside until that day.

Inside was quiet, peaceful, and safe. He would disappear into the rows for hours and read right there on the floor, back propped against the aisles of books. On his first day, he found *The Adventures of Huckleberry Finn* and *The Adventures of Tom Sawyer*. They were the embodiment of freedom and adventure. They didn't mind adults and regarded life with the impish whimsy all children should. They were more reckless than he would be, but they were also free.

Pam was the friendliest of the two librarians. Mrs. Hasselton was the stereotypical, crypt-quiet, gray-haired librarian with shriveled cheeks and bone-thin fingers. Pam was a forty-something, heavyset blond with a mother's heart, though she had no children of her own. She immediately took Rook under her wing the first day she saw him walk in sopping wet. He, of course, wasn't allowed to touch any books until he was dry, so she sat him down on a chair next to her desk and asked what he was doing there. Although she exuded kindness and gentility, he didn't talk immediately. Adults were untrustworthy creatures.

"Fine. You don't have to talk. This is a library, after all." She spoke quietly with a warm, genuine smile.

He remained quiet.

She sighed. "But do you want to know a secret?"

Wary of the secrets of adults, he simply studied her expression. Her face was full and mostly spared from wrinkles, aside from several laugh lines. Her blue eyes sparkled as they studied him.

"Librarians are the best at listening. I'm just as good at listening as I am at reading." Her smile didn't lose one degree of warmth.

He still didn't give her the chance.

On her desk was the usual assortment of pens and pencils in a mesh can, paper clips, sticky notes, a highlighter, a pad of paper, and a jar of small, foil-wrapped chocolates. He eyed the chocolates hungrily, his sweet tooth aching. He didn't get many, if any, treats living with Jackie and Lynn.

Pam noticed him glancing furtively at the jar. "I'll tell you what. If you help me organize these books on my cart here, I'll give you two pieces of chocolate."

She had a cart laden with books on the other side of her desk.

Organize a few books, get chocolate, and stay away from home? He struggled to see the down side to this woman. She hadn't said much, but in extending a task to him, she showed a willingness to trust him. He figured he could take the risk and provide her the same courtesy. It wasn't like she could do anything worse to him than had already been done. "Okay."

It was then, at the cart, that she introduced him to Huck and Tom. His reading skills were still developing at that point, but he read enough the first day to know he wanted to read more. He started going back to see Pam on more than just the rainy days, and before long, started going to the library every day. It took several trips and some help from Pam on the difficult words, but he finished Huck and Tom's adventures, twice. Pam was astounded to find he had never been read *Peter Pan*, so she showed him Neverland and the Lost Boys. His thirst for distant worlds and magical adventures grew and grew. Eventually she turned him on to Edmond Dantes in *The Count of Monte Cristo*. He admired the perseverance Dantes showed, but it was the vengeance that excited him most. The novel was above his age group, but he was mature for his age and, what's more, he wanted to take the time to slowly read and understand the novel.

The more time he took to read, the more time he spent away from home, although he never dared stay out past the time Jackie got home. Sure, Jackie would still hurt him either way, but as long as he was home on time, Jackie would never suspect he was staying out all day and socializing with another adult. The library was special and so was Pam. The library was his sanctuary, and Pam was his matron, nursing his fragile psyche.

If anyone from town knew what he had been through as a child, they would have thought he was remarkably well adjusted for someone who'd lived through such trauma. Pam was different, though. She saw through his strong front. He never knew for sure, but he believed it was Pam who called Child Protective Services.

The day Jackie caught wind of Rook's new friend, he paid her a visit at the library. Rook was with his friends when they saw the police cars race by. Naturally they followed them as best they could on their bikes and ended up in front of the library. He watched as the cops escorted Jackie out in cuffs while another officer interviewed a swollen-eyed Pam on the steps. A black eye was Jackie's way of politely telling someone to back off. Rook was just happy Jackie didn't get impolite.

Seeing Pam like that on the top of those steps, Rook swore to never involve her in his mess again. Two weeks later, CPS showed up and he didn't have to worry about involving her. He was shipped off, and eventually Carol and Richard found him. The funny thing was, when Pam looked at him with her beaten face, he didn't see anger or resentment as he expected. He saw sorrow and longing behind those watery windows to the soul. She was good and genuine through and through. It was meeting someone like her, and then Carol and Richard, that gave him enough faith to survive.

"Oh, stop with the pity-poor-me crap, kid." The fat man's voice brought him away from the memory. "Hide in the deepest parts of your subconscious, cling to warm and fuzzy memories, run all you want. The world is a bad place through and through, and it's FULL of bad people. Do you think you're the only person who ever had a shitty childhood? Bahahahaha." The voice wasn't entirely the fat man anymore. Apxutaraxi's raspy hiss was seeping through. "You're pathetic and weak. Run and hide. Run and hide. RUN AND HIDE!" The fat man taunted him.

Black tendrils sprouted out of the fat man's cheeks, chest, and thighs. One even wriggled its way out through his tear duct. The Apxutaraxi and fat man mass began to rise off the mattress. He didn't swing his legs over the side or bend at the knees. Instead, his entire body floated upward, flesh sagging downward. Rook could see more tendrils down the man's back and even more sprouting from his calves. The abomination turned upright and faced Rook, still nude and writhing. Several of the smaller tendrils grew longer and, moving out in all directions, became grabbing tentacles. They slithered into the darkness and anchored the abomination. Another tentacle shot out and wrapped around Rook.

"We've reached an impasse, Rookie. There's not enough room for the both of us in here . . ."

Chapter 25

Dawn watched the heavily falling snow and thought, oddly enough, not about the life she had lived and the people she would be leaving behind, but about Skittles. The masked man had her thrown over his shoulder and was marching her down to the shore. Rook was ten feet in front of them, back turned, and intent on whatever she had been kidnapped for. He hadn't said a word for the last fifteen minutes. She ought to have been concerned with whatever he was planning for the last few minutes of her life, but all she could think about was Skittles the cat.

Skittles was her cat as a little girl, a black and white mix-breed with white on the tip of her tiny nose and sharp green eyes. Dawn spent many summer days playing on the patio with Skittles. Skittles had a small ball of string she would chase and bat at for hours, and she would climb into Dawn's lap and curl up right on her sundress when she colored. Dawn would color for hours before she got bored and got her dolls out. Skittles was even patient enough to allow her to pretend she was a valiant steed for Barbie. Skittles wasn't a source of thrills and adrenaline; she was just nice.

Dawn considered kicking and fighting her way off the man's shoulder, but it wouldn't do any good since she was tied. She would, at best, fall to the ground into the snow-covered gravel road, and obtain several bumps, cuts, and scrapes before the man picked her up again. If she did manage to roll away before he could grab her, she would quickly freeze to death, covered in snow and unable to protect herself from the elements.

There was only one access point to the lake where there was a single dock and small boathouse. The boathouse served as a base of operations during tourist season. Sightseers and adventurers would come to the lake, and the boathouse provided tours and, of course, merchandising. Adjacent to the boathouse was a canoe trailer, racks full. Tourists could canoe the immediate vicinity or take a guided tour to Wizard Island for a day's stay using a miniature ferry designed specifically for the lake.

This time of year was extremely dangerous due to the snow's propensity to pile up fast and high. Hypothermia was also a sure bet for anyone unfortunate enough to fall into the lake. There would have been barriers such as a locked gate set up to keep ignorant adventurers out, but they didn't stop Rook and the masked man. The masked man simply disengaged the lock on the gate by smashing it.

Nodding at the canoes stored on the trailer, Rook said to the masked man, "Be a pal, would you? I have to keep one hand on Rook and one on this little lady here." He grabbed her chin.

The masked man set Dawn down at Rook's feet and went to the canoes. He effortlessly ripped the straps holding one canoe down and hoisted it off its rack.

Rook looked at her with eyes like used coffee grains, fragmented and dark, yet burning. They weren't the same eyes that looked at her longingly at the diner, filled with thought and imagination. He had referred to himself in the third person once again, too. He was clearly suffering from multiple personality disorder or a bad case of schizophrenia. There was something wrong with his circulation, too. She could see the veins in his neck and cheeks right at the surface of his skin, and they were black.

The snow soaked her jeans and stung her skin with its frigid bite. *At least I got one thing going for me,* she thought. *I was wearing jeans when he kidnapped me. I'd have frostbite already if I was wearing my PJs.*

Her jeans, she still had a lighter in her jeans. She

couldn't reach it yet, but at least she had something. Rook, or whoever was speaking at the time, said they wanted her kicking and screaming when the held her down. As soon as they untied her, she could grab it. She wasn't sure what good it would do, but it was better than nothing.

Rook had given her the lighter standing behind Shelby's. It was a custom-made, heavy, silver piece with a strong flame that shot up over an inch and a half. She'd used it since, but there should have been enough fluid remaining to ignite a good flame.

The masked man heaved the canoe into the water next to a small dock. It splashed violently and then settled on the surface. He squatted down to grab it before it could float away.

"Your chariot awaits." Rook smiled. His gums were pale gray and the saliva between his teeth was as black as his veins.

She watched as he pulled out a jade pocketknife.

"It would feel so good to cut you right now." He tilted his head back and inhaled deeply, eyes closed, savoring the thought. "I could slide it in, right between your legs . . ." He licked his lips. "Then I could cut you right up the belly like a fish, right between your breasts, take a look at you from the inside."

Not wanting to give him the opportunity, she pulled at her ropes as hard as she could and fell to her side. She thought she heard a piercing wale in the distance, shrieking then silent, shrieking then silent.

"Hahahahaha. Come here, girl." He planted his feet on either side of her and flipped her upright again.

She watched, helpless, as he lowered the knife between her legs. She screamed so loud it felt like bits of her throat were being blown into her gag. Tears poured down her face.

He held the knife at her crotch for a full minute, delighting in her screams. Then he pulled the knife up and cut through the ropes tied around her feet. "Get up, bitch. I'm not carrying you."

Her legs fell from their hog-tied position and landed flat on the ground. She lay there for a minute, composing herself, desperate for a plan. Her hands were still bound.

"I said get up," he hissed impatiently.

She rose to her feet, but he quickly spun her around and put the knife to her throat. With a whisper into her ear, he said, "Behave and I'll make it quick." He kissed the side of her neck, moaned softly with pleasure, and moved the knife to the small of her back.

She walked toward the canoe while the masked man watched silently. The large hunting knife at his waist was cached with blood, but she could see the handle was as black as his mask.

Sirens pierced through the falling snow. At first just a dull hum, then louder until it was evident they were headed toward them.

He marched her to the dock and instructed the masked man, "Stay back and take care of the cop. I'll handle her."

With another nudge in the back with the knife, Dawn moved to the end of the dock. Whether by Divine Providence or good luck, there was a gas can that had been abandoned there. She silently thanked whoever it was that had been absent-minded or lazy. When Rook turned to give the police car a second glance, she kicked the can into the canoe.

The police car rumbled down the path toward them, and skidded to a stop, kicking up gravel through the snow. From the dock it was impossible to tell who exactly was in the police car, but she could see a man in the vehicle and a large, brown creature that bounced wildly in the passenger's seat.

Rook turned back and glared at her, knife still digging into the flesh of her back. His eyes burned with anger. Things were coming apart at the seams. He jabbed the knife into her side and pushed her into the boat.

Over her muffled screams of pain, he instructed the masked man one last time, "Give us a push."

Floating above the frigid water, Dawn watched the blood seep through her fingers at her side. She had seen people get stabbed in movies thousands of times, but never realized it hurt so badly. The pain paralyzed her.

Rook paddled the canoe toward the center of the lake, cursing and grunting as they grew farther and farther from shore. "Through you, my brothers and I will have flesh," he said, grunting between strokes. Spittle flew from between his clenched teeth.

Gunshots clapped like thunder back on shore. Dawn raised her head over the edge of the canoe with a wince. Things had grown blurry, but she could see the police officer had his weapon drawn, and the masked man had his knife in hand. The furry, brown creature was on all fours, a dog. She could hear barking.

Rook jabbed her in her wounded side with an oar, and she collapsed back into the canoe with another scream of pain. "No one can save you. You're not going anywhere." He stopped and then laughed. "Well, you're going to the bottom of the lake."

She curled up on her side, facing away from him, and worked her fingers into her pocket. The ropes on her hands made it impossible to reach far enough in. She could feel the lighter on her fingertips. She would have to bring her hips in closer, stretching the wound at her side.

The smell of gasoline hung around the canoe like a swarm of mosquitoes hungry for blood. The leaking gasoline had pooled in the center of the canoe, between them, turning the accumulating snow into slush. Rook was so caught up in his moment that he was oblivious.

With another scream of pain, she curled tighter and brought her hip pocket close enough to reach the lighter. The ten seconds it took to grip the lighter between her fingers were the most excruciating of her life. She quickly closed her hand around it, afraid she would pass out from the pain and drop the lighter.

The canoe wobbled and Rook was at her back. "What have we here?" He rolled her over, splashing her legs in the gas he now crouched in. His knife was at the ready once more.

She kept her eyes on the knife and her fist around the lighter.

"Tisk tisk tisk. Were you going to light us both on fire? Did you not think I could smell that gasoline?" He lowered the knife, to her face this time. "You can't go killing yourself. That's my job. I have to send you to the bottom, the way Chief Klamath did when he created us. Then our REAL father will give us forms of our own." He stomped his feet up and down giddily. The canoe rocked in warning. "Whoa. We'd better be careful. I don't want to go overboard with you." He cackled. "Say, would you like to meet my real father? He's waiting for you down there."

He pointed down into the lake, but she had a feeling he meant much farther down than the lake. He cut the gag from her mouth and hoisted her to her feet. His eyes were no longer a fragmented, dark brown. They were solid black. He held her hands tightly. So tight her knuckles felt like they'd fracture into pieces.

"He's the harbinger of death, pain, suffering, fear . . ." He smiled wickedly. "Me."

She couldn't move her hands in position to roll the flint on the lighter.

"And you want to know the kicker? My brothers and I, we are him as he is us. Kind of like the Trinity, except with infinite numerals." His grin widened and tore the corners of Rook's mouth. His breath smelled of rotting flesh. Rook was being transformed the closer she got to a watery grave.

"Klamath opened his son's hearts and minds to us, to me. His sons, though, they were tough. We tried to kill Klamath through them, but at the last minute, with their blades to his throat and his servants dead, the chief asked for death. He wanted them to kill him. He regretted killing their whore mother. The blinding rage we had swelled up inside them fell away like scales before their eyes. Grief-stricken with guilt and reminded of the love of their mother, the sons left Klamath to live his days. They even managed to find a way to remove us! Remove anger, fear, sorrow, can you imagine? They lead their own tribe into nonexistence with their pacifistic ways! Their greatest mistake, however, was imprisoning us in artifacts. Isolated and unaffected by the love and compassion and hope you humans all cling to inside, we grew strong and became beings all our own. No longer were we a disease of the heart and mind born of that Greatest Evil. We had been made tangible. They cast us into the depths, as their mother had been. The thing about this lake, though, is that it feeds several underground springs."

"You're fucking crazy." She spat in his face.

Unperturbed, he held her wrists with one crushing hand and used the other to wipe her spit away. Licking her saliva off his fingers, he continued, "One such spring dumped into a stream a few miles from here. That stream, sluiced by heavy rains, surged and surged. It was a Hell of a storm." The tears in his mouth bled as he continued to grin and place emphasis on Hell. "You see what I'm getting at here? We were meant to be freed and spread. So much happened so we would be here today. The End of Days comes because of US. We are War, Pestilence, Famine, and Death. We're ALL the horsemen of the apocalypse. We will claim this world and remove you, you favored creatures."

With strength like the masked man's, he lifted her over the water and single-handedly held her by the neck without strain, crushing her windpipe as he babbled.

"One of those hikers found two of the artifacts. My brothers quickly went to work. He was a strong specimen to begin with, but they twisted him into the wondrous behemoth you had the pleasure of meeting on our little drive here. His name was Rudy, and he proved an excellent vessel. They searched for me with Rudy, and came oh-so-close, but then I was still too weak to call to my brothers. My artifact, on the other hand, was found by Rookie. He's been . . . interesting. You wouldn't believe how twisted he already was. Through trauma his mind had been sculpted into something magnificent. It's a shame he has to die. I would've loved to poke around in there some more, but I have a body of my own to get into!"

She looked deep into the pitch-black eyes before her and choked out a final response. "Rook, if you really are in there somewhere . . ." She paused to collect a breath. "I'm sorry." She ignited the lighter she had positioned in her hand while he ranted.

Chapter 26

Before he even opened his eyes, he sensed the nightmare around him. Tatum could feel hot, wet blood streaming down from his scalp and his shoulder stung harshly where the hunting knife had sliced through. He could hear a small crowd around him and felt hands checking for a pulse at his neck. Someone's ear was hovering directly above his mouth.

The ear-hoverer shouted, "He's alive and breathing!"

"Sue." He found words before he found sight. "Help Sue."

In the distance he heard a woman, though it wasn't Sue. "This one didn't make it."

He had watched her die, and yet, hearing it confirmed from someone else's mouth made him wish he wasn't waking up.

He opened his eyes and saw a blinding white light. The ear-hoverer and the woman in the distance were gone.

"Tatum," the light spoke.

It sounded like Jon. A flash of pain exploded in the back of his head and then disappeared.

He cried out and sat up. The light was a flashlight, not as bright as before. Ear-hoverer and distant woman were both standing by him now. Several other people from the neighborhood circled around him.

"Take it easy there, deputy. You were assaulted." Ear-hoverer placed a hand on his good shoulder. "Don't get up yet."

From the back of his mind, where the pain had originated in the flash, came Tank and Crater Lake. He had to get the dog and get to the lake, immediately. He would find the masked man there. He would kill the man.

The ear-hoverer tried to hold him down but loosened his grip once he figured that Tatum would do more harm to himself struggling than standing. Ear-hoverer was a narrow man with a big stomach. He smelled like smoke. The distant woman was a pale blond with her hair in a ponytail. They were the EMTs who he had shipped off Mitchell Henderson. He had been unconscious for a while. He couldn't waste anymore time.

"Wait. Hold on, deputy. We have to get you fixed up." The ear-hoverer held his arm as he tried to push by.

"I'm fine. I need to go after the suspect!" He pulled his arm away. "You two take care of Sue." He choked back tears that tried to well up. There would be a time for tears, but for now, he had an immediate purpose. "And get help from Berryville down here now!"

He floored the cruiser all the way to Rook's cabin, cherries blazing. He wanted to be with Sue, but there was nothing he could do for her now. The EMTs would take care of her body and he would say his good-byes later.

He wasn't sure how he knew, but Tank would be an integral part in whatever was going to happen at the lake. He just had to make sure the icy roads didn't kill them before they made it.

The cruiser slid to a stop in front of Rook's cabin. The moment he stepped out, he could hear Tank howling inside. He envisioned Tank leaping on to him and tearing him apart in a maddened frenzy. Fortunately, when he opened the door, Tank instead ran past him and into the open door of the cruiser. The chocolate lab placed his paws on the dashboard and barked at him to hurry.

Tatum sped forty miles over the speed limit, only ever slowing to negotiate the turns. Even cutting his speed in half, the ice made every one of his turns a roll of the dice. One especially bad patch of ice and his car would barrel roll right into the woods.

Tank swayed in his half squat in the passenger's seat, his tail wrapped under his stomach. His heightened senses may have primed him for whatever lay ahead, but the finer points of gravity still eluded him. He curled up on the seat and then stood again, unable to find his comfort zone.

"Sorry, pal. We have to go fast. You understand, don't you?" He alternated between looking at the road and looking at the dog.

Tank stared him down and chuffed.

"Like you could drive better."

The closer to the lake they got, the eerier the forest around them seemed. Daylight was making its first appearance over the horizon beyond the treetops. Night fought to hang on. The ice became a heavy snow on a deathly quiet landscape. The world was in transition and there was another, more sinister transition to be made. He didn't know how he knew, but the masked man, Dawn, and Rook were at the lake. The light had told him somehow.

He left the sirens on as he approached the lake. They had served to alert the few motorists he passed and would now alert the masked man and company, but there was no need for stealth. Tiptoeing around would only waste precious time. Back up, however, would be most beneficial. In his hurry, he hadn't thought to call units to the lake. He picked up the CB radio, the same one he had talked to Rose on less than twenty-four hours before she was murdered, and, after observing a brief moment of silence, radioed Berryville.

The gate blocking the entrance to the boat ramp and dock area was wide open. The chain that had been wrapped between the bars of the gate had been torn apart and the lock smashed and discarded to the side. Once through the gate, Tatum picked up speed. He could see Rook, Dawn, and the masked man. Tank barked wildly and scratched at the door.

He rocketed down the small slope toward them and slammed on the brakes, but the tires failed to grab the gravel under the snow and instead slid uncontrolled. Fearing he'd overshoot right into them, he jammed the wheel to the left and the car spun, kicking up the gravel it finally found. From their perspective his maneuver probably seemed deliberate. He would've laughed to himself had Rook not pushed a tied Dawn into a canoe at that very moment. The masked man pushed them off, stood up, and wasted no time moving swiftly toward him.

He grabbed the cruiser's shotgun from its wedged position and flung open his door. Before he could get out, Tank squeezed past him and jumped out of the car.

"Damn it, Tank! No!"

The dog was on his own, to serve whatever reason he had been brought along now.

Tatum dropped into a squat behind the hood of his cruiser and pointed the shotgun on the masked man.

"Rudy!" Tatum shouted.

The masked man stopped in his tracks.

"Rudy Bustwick!" He fought the impulse to pull the trigger straight away. "If you're still in there, now is your chance. Drop the weapon and get down on the ground. You only get one warning this time." He cocked the gun to show he meant business. In the distance he could see Rook rowing the canoe farther into the lake.

Rudy had swelled up larger than the six foot nine that had been listed on his driver's license, but Tatum was sure it was him behind the mask. He didn't fully understand what was going on, but he knew something supernatural was afoot. The light had shown him. In some way, Jon had shown him. He could feel it.

Stopped for a second, as if the name had triggered a sole synapse to fire, only to be squelched by thousands of other synapses firing against it, Rudy resumed his charge.

Susan Wzorek had been a dear friend, a mentor, and a lover. He had been training in his hometown, desiring to get a position there, when she was brought in as the new sheriff. She trained him, pushed him, and shared with him her experiences as an officer of the law. He respected her, and she saw in him the same ambitious spirit she had once shared in her field.

Their relationship grew from strictly professional to something more. They admired one another. Still, she wouldn't give him the job as her deputy. He was a trainee, and she was notoriously tough. He also knew she simply just enjoyed having him jump at her every whim, which he would do anyway. When Deputy Driggs accidentally put a bullet through his own kneecap into his tibia, her hand was forced. She called him into her office, and when she broke the news, he exclaimed he'd never been happier to hear a friend shot himself in the leg. They laughed, and in the joy of the moment, he hugged her. When their bodies touched, he felt electricity tingling and heard birds singing all at once. He kissed her without thinking, and she didn't shrink away. The electricity grew to full-on lightning, shooting sparks between them and the birds became a choir. From then on, regardless of their professional relationship and their difference in age, it was impossible to deny what they had between them.

He would never feel her electricity again, and what was worse, they had never shared their love with anyone, though rumors had abounded. If he managed to survive, it would be like they never happened. That love would simply disappear.

He squeezed the trigger.

Tank, poised to attack the gruesome man and barking all the while, was silenced by the explosive shotgun blast.

The masked man absorbed the shot like a giant sponge made of meat.

Tatum knew the buckshot had dug deep, squarely in the center of the man's chest, and yet the man was simply knocked backwards, not down. He fired a second shot without hesitating.

The masked man fell to one knee. Even with an enhanced ability to eat bullets like hotcakes, his body could only take so much.

Tatum rose from his defensive position, gun still sighted on the man. He thought about Mike on the football field, standing five yards out from the wide receiver before a snap. Mike had a knack for getting underneath and had recorded more interceptions and defensive touchdowns than any other player in the history of the division. On the field he was called Mr. Pick-Six. He wouldn't have any more nicknames. Tatum wanted to unload the rest of his twelve-gauge.

Tank growled. The fur on his back bristled into a jagged ridge. Keeping his eyes on Rudy, he backed around, toward the shore. He wanted to go for Rook in the canoe. Tatum could see it in the dog's movement.

Rudy's hands were dug deep into the snow beside him.

"We tried to take you into custody, but you killed Sue. Then you attacked again here. I am completely clear to kill you." Tatum stepped closer to get a clean head shot. He figured having nothing more than a spinal stump jutting out from his neck would stop Rudy.

He heard a splash and looked up to see Tank had gone into the frigid water after the canoe. Tank was better insulated, but was still subject to hypothermia.

"Tank, no!" he cried out.

Rudy seized his opportunity. Hands full of gravel and dirt, he blinded Tatum. The behemoth wasn't beyond dirty fighting. He charged, head down like a rhino, and plunged his massive shoulder deep into Tatum's gut.

Shielding his eyes from the debris, Tatum vomited air when Rudy hit him in the stomach. The monstrosity lifted him from the ground and slammed him down on the hood of the car. His shotgun disappeared into the snow on the ground beside them. He saw the glint of the large hunting knife above him and rolled to the side, narrowly dodging the blade as it plunged through the hood of the car. The metal shrieked as it had when Sue was killed. Screaming with adrenaline, Tatum, still on his back on the hood, lunged forward and swung with all his might.

Rudy jerked back to free the hunting knife, not afraid of the fist flying toward him, but dodged it inadvertently. His mask peeled away like a hardened scab, revealing bloody, pale tissue beneath. Tatum's fist had snagged and ripped away the mask, rather than impacting his face with any direct force.

Every vein and every capillary in his face was black. They formed an all-encompassing net around what little white tissue remained. Tatum was reminded of the moss like weeds he had pulled from his uncle's lake while fishing the bottom for catfish. His hook would come up with hunks of the sludge-cached weeds, twined together by hundreds of tiny stems. Rudy's face consisted of hundreds of similar stems, each connecting to another in a web of darkness over bloated flesh. What had appeared to be a trick of his mask turned out to be true nothingness in his eyes. There were only empty sockets where his eyes ought to be. The unseen force that had been guiding him, the supernatural presence, hadn't a need for ocular organs. How or why they had been removed, Tatum didn't care to find out.

Turned berserker by the loss of his mask, the beast sunk his hunting knife deep into Tatum's already damaged shoulder. Leaving the knife embedded in Tatum's body and the vehicle, the enraged murderer punched him hard enough to break three ribs.

Tatum gasped for breath as his broken bones poked at his lungs. Each shallow breath felt like a dagger. The world around him shrunk and spun. Each remaining heartbeat pulsed less and less oxygenated blood throughout his system. His muscles trembled and weakened. The periphery of his vision blurred, but he saw something remarkable.

The man who was pure rage had stood up straight, shoulders heaving as he panted, and raised his fists above his head in one clenched mass meant to smash Tatum's skull in with the force of a wrecking ball. Poised to deliver the killing blow, Rudy was suddenly wrapped by darkness, like Death's cloak.

Tatum closed his eyes, waiting for his turn.

Death sounded strangely like the wings of a great bird flapping wildly.

He opened his eyes and, through the blur, saw what was, in fact, a large, black bird. An enormous raven had set upon Rudy. Its wings beat savagely around him as it pecked out tufts of hair and bits of his scalp. The raven had one snow-white feather, which would have seemed remarkable on any other day, but Tatum had already seen so much this day.

Tatum didn't think a bird should bother such a beast, but Rudy was markedly perturbed by it.

While one raven kept Rudy busy batting, a second raven swooped down to pick up the mask in its talons. In one swift move, it clutched the mask and carried it toward the lake, dropping it into the deep waters.

Out on the lake Rook was standing in the canoe, holding Dawn. Tatum couldn't black out, couldn't disappear into the oblivion he had been knocked into before, into the oblivion Rudy's empty sockets previewed. Maybe there was something on the other side, beyond oblivion. He so wanted to close his eyes one last time and drift away to find out, but he couldn't. Dawn depended on him. Rook depended on him. There was still hope. There had to be.

Screaming through clenched teeth, he gripped the knife in his free hand and pulled with all his might. At first it didn't budge, but then, with a sudden creak, it gave way. The teeth of the blade scraped against the metal and then through the meat of his shoulder. He growled in pain, feeding on the adrenaline that his body released. At last the blade came completely free and exited both the hood and his shoulder.

He rolled off the hood and fell to his knees. The pain in his ribs was excruciating. However, the pain focused his weakening body. One arm dangling, he pushed himself to his feet, using his clenched fist on the ground. The knife was heavy and warm. It radiated energy like pavement on a hot summer day. It filled him with strength. It felt dangerously good.

The attacking raven squawked wildly once Rudy finally wrapped one of his massive hands around it. His thumb, forefinger, and middle finger were around the bird's neck. His other two fingers were tucked under one of the struggling wings. He held it at arm's length and squeezed, intending to pop the bird's head clean off.

With Rudy turned away from him, Tatum wasted

no time and plunged the knife as far as he could downward into his neck, angled toward the jugular. He could feel the blade serrate against Rudy's collarbone. Rudy dropped the frantic bird, which flew away miraculously unfazed, and fell to his knees.

The knife called to Tatum, begging to be plunged into Rudy again and again. He resisted the urge to grab the knife once more and instead reached for his shotgun.

Rudy collapsed backwards, over his bent legs, and unfolded flat against the ground. Blood spurted from his neck and multiple bullet wounds. His body could take no more punishment.

Tatum took no chances and pressed the shotgun against Rudy's forehead. He felt no guilt or shame. He knew the real Rudy had died long ago. Holding his breath, he fired the shotgun and watched Rudy's distorted face turn into nothing more than a smear on the ground. The snow all around them was stained red and black.

One of the ravens returned and landed on what remained of Rudy's skull. Feathers ruffled, some missing, white still intact, it was the same raven he had just saved. It tore at the flesh around the knife, gripped the handle with its talons, and beat its wings wildly to pull the weapon out.

The spectacle merited attention, but he still had lives to save.

When he saw the canoe, he feared he was too late. It had become one enormous fireball over the water.

Chapter 27

Rook wanted to run and hide, exactly like the fat man told him, but he couldn't. The road he had traveled to get away from his past, to escape his demons, had come to an end. His demons, along with a few new ones, had caught up to him. The most lethal of which had him wrapped in tentacles that smelled like gasoline.

The fat man abomination had gone silent. His eyes were open, his threatening expression unchanged, yet he was motionless. Only his tentacles wriggled, as with a mind of their own. Something was substantially distracting Apxutaraxi in the tangible world, leaving Rook bound and alone in the presence of his greatest fear.

He had never wanted to see the fat man again. He tried to forget him, to bury him where he could never be brought up again, to block all access to the man, to repress him. Nothing can stay repressed forever, especially not when the essence of Evil itself is rooting around in your head.

If he ran, what then? He could run and run, deeper and deeper into his subconscious to the point where he'd never emerge in the real world again. He'd be completely catatonic if it weren't for Apxutaraxi at the controls.

That wasn't an option.

He had to regain control. He had to fight.

The gasoline smell intensified. Arms pinned to his sides, his nose and lungs burned as he breathed in the air wafting up from the tentacles around him.

"I'm not going to run from you. I will never run again!

Do you hear me?!" He knew Apxutaraxi could hear him. Whether sharing the same corner of his mind or on a canoe with Dawn, Apxutaraxi could hear him.

Rook could see the canoe. He could see his hands wrapped around Dawn's neck. He fought Apxutaraxi to loosen them.

Back with the fat man. The tentacles tightened around him. Fire flickered behind the frozen eyes.

"You're going to fight? I'm in the middle of something here!" Apxutaraxi spoke through the fat man and slammed Rook against the bed, where he had hovered. He closed four chubby fingers and a thumb into a tight fist. The springs of the bed wrapped him and squeezed tight, cutting into him like barbed wire. Broken by the fat man, the mattress swallowed Rook. It smelled like the fat man—boiled eggs, sweat, and pine.

"No!" Rook screamed. Not in fear, but in resistance. "NEVER again!" A shock wave, detonated from a payload of nuclear emotion, internalized and welled up over a lifetime, exploded out from him and splintered the bed in all directions.

This was HIS mind, HIS body. He would be damned if he rolled over and let Apxutaraxi run him deep into the recesses of his own psyche. He couldn't run anymore. He wouldn't.

"I REALLY don't have time for this, Rookie!" No longer burdened in the fat man's style of speech, Apxutaraxi's words scratched out of his throat like tires on sandy asphalt. Every word was abrasive. "Do you forget, boy? Your anger feeds me!"

Two tentacles shot out, seeking to reclaim Rook like leeches.

Raising his own hand, he stopped them mid-air. This was his realm, not Apxutaraxi's. He jerked his hand in a tearing motion and the tentacles ripped from the fat man. "It's not anger."

Dawn. Apxutaraxi was talking. His hands were still around her neck. He was going to drown her.

The fat man again.

Breaking the surface of still, conscious waters only

to be pulled back down and submerged in sub-consciousness. In a lethal gesture, he choked the air in front of him and the fat man gargled. He would crush the fat man's throat and make it known he would never fear him again. He would destroy the manifestation and control the memory. The fat man's eyes bulged and his cheeks turned red, then purple, then blue. Rook felt waves of pleasure.

Dawn. He was choking her. He was physically choking her. Not imagining the fat man in his own head, he was really, truly choking the life out of his friend. Him, Rook Evrett. Not Apxutaraxi.

Apxutaraxi had subsided though he knew this was the eye of the storm. Apxutaraxi was far from done. He was just revving up.

Before he could react, Dawn garbled out an apology. "Rook, if you really are in there somewhere . . ." She paused. "I'm sorry."

In the next several seconds, time seemed to leave its linear path and loop around in what felt like hours. The flame, though it burned feverishly on the fumes, didn't ignite the gasoline immediately, but it would once she dropped it into the pool in the canoe. He dropped her into the water, her best chance given the situation, and watched the lighter fall. He wanted to burn. Apxutaraxi might have lived on somehow, but he was willing to chance it. He wanted Apxutaraxi to burn with him, as they had burned at Jon's. He would burn for Jon, for Rose, for Driggs, for Mike, for everybody who had died.

Apxutaraxi, reinvigorated and infuriated, seized control and plucked the lighter from the air with the accuracy and agility of a ninja surpassing his sensei's practiced palm. Still upright and unaffected in the rapid movement, the flame danced mockingly. Rook felt the corner of his mouth rise into a satisfied smirk.

Water splashed over the side of the boat as Dawn disappeared into the lake.

From his peripheral he saw a large, black raven swoop down full of intent. Spinning, lighter still burning determinedly in hand, he looked beyond the raven to the shore where Tatum and the no-longer-masked man were engaged in combat. A second raven was also coming toward him, mask in talons, and a third floated in circles above the fight. Both he and Apxutaraxi shared this assessing reaction. He felt no resistance but fluidity in the movement, as if two sets of joints were swiveling him around.

The mutual movement accomplished little in the way of preparedness. Without time to react, the dive-bombing raven hit its target. The guided missile of feathers, bone, and keratin knocked the lighter and its eager flame out of his hand. This time the ninja was too late and the gasoline sensei retained his prize.

As the flames spread across the canoe and upward around him with the rapidity of a hungry cheetah, he saw Dawn kicking herself to the surface, gasping for air.

In a reaction of both survival instinct and will to kill, Apxutaraxi lunged out of the canoe toward her. The icy water doused the flames, but his legs still burned. Being pulled down to the depths by yet another unseen force, Apxutaraxi clung to her, desperate to evade his tomb with her death in order to gain his freedom in the final minute.

It felt as if the lady of the lake, Chief Klamath's wife, Apxutaraxi's mother in some twisted way, was dragging them to the depths with a siren's call, a siren's call that felt like a two-ton lead weight in his pocket.

Rook smiled.

Apxutaraxi did have control on most of their drive out—most, but not all. Between the segments of time he lost entirely, when they were trading in the stolen cruiser for his pickup, he had the presence of mind to pocket the obsidian wolf, the item Apxutaraxi had gone back to the station to retrieve. He couldn't leave it behind. He needed it with him, under his watchful eye for as long as he journeyed the world and spread evil like a plague. And yet, he didn't want it on the lake. Apxutaraxi had intended to keep it close but safely locked in the glove compartment, unknown to Rook. He had dismissed Rook as too confused and caught up in the whirlwind to piece the importance of the artifact together. That was Rook's greatest weapon in his fight.

He had been underestimated time and time again by Apxutaraxi, and deservedly so. Apxutaraxi had bent him to his will and tortured him inside his own mind. Rook had focused himself, and, while being genuinely tormented beyond his control, reached out into the real world and pilfered away the wolf. Apxutaraxi thought he had locked it away in the glove box, but Rook had planted the memory for Apxutaraxi and hid away the truth, until now, the same way he had repressed his other memories. He locked it away in a separate corner of his mind. His mind was special, after all.

How, how did you?!

Rook disregarded Apxutaraxi's questioning and communicated his own thoughts. "Let her go!" He fought against Apxutaraxi with the power he found against the fat man. Apxutaraxi was much stronger at full attention, though.

Dawn sunk with them. Held by the ankle, Rook watched as the last bubbles of life escaped her lips and water filled her lungs.

She dies with you!

The water grew darker around them. The morning's rays struggled to penetrate as deep as they had sunk. Icy death embraced them.

Then, splashing. The kicking of legs and paddling of arms. Above Dawn's motionless body a brown blur, a speck on the surface pulling her back toward the light.

She would never be successfully pulled up as long as Apxutaraxi, and the weight of an ancient force, dragged them down.

The speck, that familiar brown, four-legged dog was paddling vehemently. Loyalty, hope, friendship to the end, all rolled up in one furry package. An image of Tank as a puppy in his basket flashed before Rook's eyes again.

"LET GO OF HER!" Rook commanded, and his hand obeyed its true master.

Even after releasing, his hand waived frantically,

trying to find her ankle once more, but she was moving upward, the air trapped in her body lifting her to Tank, and they were moving downward—endlessly—to depths in the crater no man had ever seen.

I am stronger than you! I will have my form free of that damned artifact!

He felt Apxutaraxi raging inside of him, like a madman throwing himself against the walls of the asylum. Devoid of breath, his lungs greeted water in the same way Dawn's had. He watched his own bubbles of life leave him. Tentacles ripped out of his skin. His veins were tearing themselves away from his body, starting with the hand that had first touched the carving. Apxutaraxi was physically tearing away from him, gaining form. He noticed the carving in his other hand. Apxutaraxi had taken it from his pocket.

***

Darkness. Complete and inescapable. He was inside his mind again. His body had been given to the scythe of Death. He knew these moments were the last firings of synapses in his brain, frantically trying to preserve itself.

Apxutaraxi was in the darkness.

He felt weightless, no longer pulled or pushed against his will. A weight had been loosened from him.

"Rookie, Rookie, Rookie."

Apxutaraxi appeared before him in the form of his father, Jackie. Tall, thick, calloused, the boxer before him was his father as he had last seen him, with missing teeth, dried blood, a stubble chin, and mane of dark, greasy hair like that of a lion—except, he was twisted by Apxutaraxi. Gone were his cracked lips, replaced by a full view of his black gums and missing teeth. He had a perpetual grin. His fists, if they were still fists, looked gloved, but were, in fact, massively calloused, as if he had been ceaselessly smashing skulls for the fifteen-plus years he had been dead. His skin was nearly transparent and glistened with sweat. Every black vein in his body showed through. His eyes, once blue and full of lies, were speckled with black, like leeches were swimming in his ocular fluid.

"What? You don't like how I look now? Come on, give Daddy a hug!"

He disappeared, reappeared in front of Rook, and swung one of the mighty, calloused fists.

Rook floated to the right, avoiding the blow with ease.

"You thought you could get the better of me with your little tricks and your outburst against the fat man." The words poured out of Jackie, though he had no lips and his Adam's apple did not stir. He appeared behind Rook this time and slugged him directly in the spine. "You thought the fat man was your greatest fear. Well, I got news for you, Rookie. I am every fear and I am your greatest. I am fear and I am you." He laughed through his lip-less smile as Rook fell. "Now I don't know how you overcame my fat man, but it's time for you to die."

Knocked to the ground by the second blow, Rook caught himself and spun around, holding the same Browning A-Bolt II that had failed to kill Jackie before. The gun was loaded this time.

"Love." Rook revealed his ammunition. "Your antithesis. The same force that imprisoned you before. It may be trite, but it's true. In spite of all the evils in this world, all the evils I've encountered, in spite of you . . ." He paused and dodged another blow. ". . . I still have love in me. I love my friends, I love my dog, and, I recently discovered, I can still love myself. I ran away for years. I ran from my past and I ran from myself. I hid in a cabin and in stories and even in my own head, but you, and believe me I don't wish to give you any credit, you forced me to face my past and find myself."

Apxutaraxi growled and swung a quick backhand at him.

He dodged once more, determined not to get hit again before he could get a good shot off. "You cornered me, and with nowhere left to run, nowhere left to hide, nothing left to lose, I discovered that I want to be Rook Evrett. I want to be a writer named after Richard and Carol Evrett. I want a life with people in it. Good people, like Tatum and Dawn. And I deserve it. Adversity hasn't made me some distorted shell, meant to be buried under the earth, hidden for the rest of my life, only to emerge at the end." He fired the words like bullets and pulled the trigger. "I want to live!"

At point blank range he didn't miss. The bullets tore through Apxutaraxi.

The fists stopped falling.

Apxutaraxi looked down at his wounds and laughed. "Hahahahahaha! Oh my little cicada. This IS the end. I will emerge and you will die."

Chapter 28

"So when was the last time you visited him?" Dawn asked as Tatum pushed a wheelchair down the hospital hallway.

"I checked up on him after everything happened. I mean, I was here for some other things anyway." He put a hand to his shoulder, then ribs, and gave her a half-smile. "But I haven't had a chance to visit since then. I get reports, though. They say he's healthy enough for a circuit around the floor now. I figure he'll enjoy a little ride." He patted the wheelchair. "Here it is. Room 4709."

Tatum knocked and, after hearing a shout of approval, pushed the door open. He and Dawn stepped in to see a pair of feet at the end of a bed. The bathroom walls immediately to the right blocked off the rest from view.

"Hey!" Barry waved at them excitedly. "What took you so long? Get me the hell out of this place!" While his upper body bounced merrily for them, his legs remained motionless. His head was still shaved and heavily bandaged from a recent round of corrective surgery. Drainage tubes led from his lower intestine to a bag attached to one of his legs.

Dawn cringed. "I still can't get used to all that."

Tatum kept composed.

"Eh, don't worry about it. I'm on enough morphine to kill an elephant. Who knew I had a high drug tolerance?" He smiled sheepishly. "And I only have to use this bag for another week, then they're gonna finish fixing that. The wheels will take some getting used to, but at least I don't have to give up smoking due to damaged lungs." Barry grinned at her in surprisingly good spirits. He had been inconsolable when he found out Mike was dead, but since then, his entire personage had changed.

"The doctors only encouraged it," Dawn said. "I don't have any long-term damage. My lungs are just going to be irritated for a while."

"So does that mean you are going to smoke again?" Barry asked her like he was rebuilding his client base. Cogs in his head were already busy at work, finding ways to add secret compartments to his wheelchair.

She thought for a moment, and then after Tatum coughed to passively remind them of his presence, she replied, "I don't think so. This is a good opportunity for me to kick the habit."

"And I would suggest you do the same," Tatum admonished Barry.

Like a scolded child, he appeased Tatum. "Yes, Sheriff."

"I'm not officially Sheriff. I'm just the interim until the Town Council finds someone more qualified," Tatum informed him.

Both Barry and Dawn looked at him, then Barry spoke again. "After everything you went through, you don't think you're qualified?"

"You know. I don't remember you being so talkative before, Barry," Tatum humbly changed the subject.

"New lease on life. I want to be a player in the game now."

Dawn and Tatum shrugged at each other confusedly.

"Say, how is Tank?" Barry asked, holding himself up by his arms. "And are we ever going for this walk?"

Tatum smiled and brought the chair to the bedside. He tried to help Barry swing his legs, but Barry shooed him away and told him he could do it himself.

"Tank's doing better." He and Dawn watched as Barry lifted and shimmied his way into the chair, wincing only a couple times. "He made me take him to the lake a couple dozen times, but he's adjusting. The vet said he had hypothermia of sorts after he dragged Dawn out. Still, he sat there waiting for Rook to pop up. He would've paddled back out there and froze to death to save Rook. When we go, he just sits by the water, waiting for Rook to come back up."

They all went quiet.

They had lost friends, a brother, good people, and lovers. Tatum didn't speak much of Sue or Mike. He carried his pain quietly and put on a strong face for those around him. A large service was held for all the dead. Pictures were blown up and placed by the closed caskets.

Rose's picture captured her larger-than-life personality and even larger heart. She was frozen forever in time with a smile for cameraman George, whisking eggs in her kitchen, wearing an apron that asked you to kiss the cook. George was buried in the plot by her side.

Miles's family purchased him a large, ornate mausoleum all his own. Even with his aboveground resting place, above everyone else as his family indiscreetly pointed out, his casket was next to all the others for the service. One town, united hearts.

Mike's picture was one of him in full pads, helmet tucked under his arm. He gave everyone visiting his casket a huge grin. Looking at the picture, you couldn't help but wonder what mischief he'd planned for that day. He wouldn't be causing any more trouble, but he'd certainly be sitting on Barry's shoulder, egging him on as Barry lived for the both of them.

Sue's picture was from her early years on the force. Her green eyes were more brilliant and filled with life than ever. She was young and hopeful, not yet dampened by time in her profession. Every button on her pressed uniform was shined. Under her hat was the smile Tatum had been lucky enough to find. Behind her was the American flag.

Deputy Driggs was buried with the group as well. Jon was declared missing. Curiously, a large raven with a single white feather joined the burial proceedings in an unusual fashion. The crowd watched as the raven flew in low circles, spiraling down around them. It first landed on the mausoleum and then hopped casket to casket, leaving a single scratch mark from one of its talons on each. It reached Rook's last and loitered there longer. It stared at the casket for several minutes. Several mourners speculated it was studying its own reflection in the glossy acrylic on the lid. It left no mark.

For Rook they buried an empty casket. His body was never recovered from the lake. Detectives labeled him as a high-priority subject of interest, and though they came close with Driggs, they were never able to pin anything on him beyond Dawn's kidnapping. Neither she nor Tatum would testify against him anyway. Tatum told Dawn about the light and the ravens, and she told him about the multiple personalities at war. They weren't sure what had happened, but they agreed forces beyond their understanding had been at play. They didn't talk any further on the subject and preferred to remember Rook as the friend he had been. The cops had a perfectly good scapegoat in Rudy.

Dawn pulled a charred lighter out of her pocket and flicked its spent assembly to no physical result. It had been recovered on the smoldering aluminum canoe and eventually returned to her. The silver could be restored, but she hadn't yet decided what she wanted to do with it. Her lungs burned just looking at it. She had died and been brought back by CPR Tatum administered before he collapsed beside her. The three of them could've started a back-from-the-dead club, she thought to herself. Barry, Tatum, and Dawn had all been in Death's embrace, only to be released back to life. Referring once more to Tank, she restarted the conversation. "Is he getting along with Duke?"

"Of course," Tatum assured her. "They frolic around jailed hooligans all day and tear up my place at night. It took two days for Duke to turn back up after he went missing from the station. Something scared him that bad. You wouldn't know it now, though. He and Tank are a force to be reckoned with." He smiled warmly.

He wheeled Barry out of the room and the three of them walked down the hospital hallway. A midday sun burned brightly through a large window at the end of the hall.

"I hear both of you got some scars, too," Barry addressed them. "Dawn, you mind lifting your shirt and showing me yours?"

She smacked him on the shoulder.

He looked at Tatum, who was shaking his head. "Worth a shot, right?"

At the end of the hall they took a moment to look out the window and enjoy the sun making a hard January snow sparkle like millions of tiny diamonds.

Barry's stomach then had an idea. "This is nice and all, but what do you say we sneak me down to the cafeteria for a pre-dinner snack? Ever since I got my appetite back, I've had an unbelievable case of the munchies." He looked at the snow again. "How about some ice cream?"

Dawn and Tatum chuckled with him as they boarded the elevator.

***

Two thousand miles away, in a dingy studio apartment, an obese man sat back in his recliner, belly spilling over the sides. The hair on his head was long since gone, but the hair bristling out from under his stained, white wife-beater was gray. The pale glow of an old tube television rolled over his skin. A fan hummed beside him, three tassels fluttering.

A knock at the door stirred him from his zombie stare. His doorbell hadn't worked in years. With a sigh and a groan, he grabbed his cane and climbed to his feet. "Hang on!" he shouted. "I'll be right there!"

A second knock, followed by a quick third, served little more purpose than to irritate him. "Hold your damn horses, you impatient prick!" he yelled through the door.

His fat fingers struggled to pinch the chain latch and remove it. Eventually, they achieved their goal, and with a flick of the lock on the knob, the door popped open.

A skinny man with dark, shaggy hair stood before him. The man was wearing flip-flops, beige cargo shorts, a black T-shirt, sunglasses, and a golden grin. He was tickled about something.

"Who the hell are you?" he asked the man.

The man studied him and he studied back. "Holy shit! Jackie?! Is that you? I heard you were dead!"

Rather than an answer, he got a question. "Do you own the attached building? The one with the heavy metal door and red brick?"

"You aren't Jackie."

The man's smile suddenly seemed malevolent. "Nope."

"Wh-who are you?" The jovial reunion had soured. "You're his kid, aren't you!" He slammed the door shut as the mystery man extended his hand. Four fingers were crushed with an audible snap.

The mysterious man didn't flinch. He pushed the door open.

"Y-you're his fucking kid!" The obese man backed up.

"Wrong again. But I do know him. Tried to kill him, had to settle on locking him away where he'll never see light again." He paused. "Though he gets feisty every time I go near that damn town . . ." The man at the door's calm rant made no sense to the fat man.

The man at the door removed his sunglasses with his damaged hand. His blood was black. His eyes were blacker. "I'm actually killing you to see if it will shut him up for a while."

CPSIA information can be obtained
at www.ICGtesting.com
Printed in the USA
BVHW051020090723
666959BV00005B/287

9 781618 974426